CRAVING ALL HIS LOVE 2

TYRECKA LIGGONS

D1367265

SHAN PRESENTS, LLC

Published by Shan Presents
www.shanpresents.com

✾ Created with Vellum

SUBSCRIBE

Text Shan to 22828 to stay up to date with new releases, sneak peeks, contest, and more....

WANT TO BE A PART OF SHAN PRESENTS?

To submit your manuscript to Shan Presents, please send the first three chapters and synopsis to <u>submissions@shanpresents.com</u>

PROLOGUE

RAMSEY

I guess you could say I had drunk too much the night of Zay's birthday party because, days later, I still had trouble recovering. I had been throwing up like crazy since the night of the party. I didn't make it in Nanna's house good before I was throwing up everywhere, waking them up with all the noise I was making. After days of resting with no progress of getting better, I decided to pull myself out of bed to make my way to the drugstore to buy a pregnancy test to confirm what I was pretty sure I already knew. Rory had been saying the same thing since she arrived back home from the hotel with Boss, finding me lying on the couch, passed out, feeling like I was slowly dying.

I was glad Luna was with Jen. I allowed Luchi to go with Zay to hang out with Cari. I was worried he would see Zoo. I didn't want to go back to square one with Luchi, and he was finally getting to the point where he didn't ask me about Zoo every day. I knew I couldn't be selfish by keeping Luchi and Ba'Cari apart.

"Are you nervous?" Rory asked, standing in the bathroom with me, giving me no privacy. She had been on my back since I told her I was finally going to the store to purchase a pregnancy test. I was done being in denial.

"Yes, I'm nervous, but I wouldn't be too surprised if I am. It was something we planned together before things between us went south."

"How would you feel if it comes back that you are pregnant?"

"I mean, it is what it is. You know how I feel about my kids, and this one wouldn't be any different. I'm no stranger to being a single mother," I answered, squatting down over the toilet to get on with it.

I was putting on a brave face, yet so many different emotions ran through my head as Rory and I waited for the results in silence. A part of me was nervous and over thinking everything. If I was pregnant, I didn't understand why it would happen right now when we've been trying for months. A part of me was happy for Zoo, then nervousness quickly washed over me. I knew how quickly niggas could switch up. I didn't know if I was ready to be a single mother of three, but if so, I was prepared to handle my business like I had been doing.

I was already nervous enough about what I was doing, and the constant ringing of my phone wasn't helping any. Figuring answering it would help pass the time, I picked my phone up to see who was calling. Seeing that it was Jen calling, I quickly answered since she had Luna.

"Hello?" I answered as I watched Rory pick up the pregnancy test to read the results.

"It's positive," Rory mouthed to me at the same time as Jen began to cry into the phone. I was stuck on Rory telling me I was pregnant. I was telling myself I was going to be okay, but really, I was scared.

Jen quickly pulled my attention back to the phone call as she cried out to me.

"Ramsey!" she screamed into the phone. "Oh my goodness, Ramsey, I don't know... I don't know what happened!"

"Jen, calm down and tell me what's wrong. Is my daughter okay?" I asked in a panic, causing Rory to look at me, concerned.

"I'm sorry, Ramsey!" Jen cried.

"Jen, where is my fucking daughter?" I yelled. I was beginning to lose it.

"Someone, um, someone took her from the waterfront park. I only turned my head for a second, and she was gone," Jen yelled, hysterically crying. I felt as if someone had knocked the wind out of me at the same time as vomit went flying everywhere.

Was I hearing her correctly? Did that bitch just tell me someone had taken my daughter?

1

RAMSEY

"Jen, if this is some sick joke, it's not funny." I wiped the vomit that ran down my chin with the back of my hand. Sadly, I kind of wanted it to be a sick joke that she was playing. I knew better, though; something felt wrong. It was real.

"She was playing on the playground, I looked in my purse for a split second, and by the time I looked back up, she was gone," Jen yelled. I could tell she was going crazy.

"Jen, call the police. I'm on my way."

I could hear Jen breaking down before the phone went dead.

My hands trembled as I dialed Zoo's number. I could barely keep it together as I thought about the unknown.

"What?" he rudely answered on the third ring.

"Bring my fucking daughter home, right now!" I screamed into the phone.

"What the fuck are you talking about?" Zoo yelled back.

"I'm not playing with you, Zouk. Bring Luna home, right fucking now."

"Ramsey, I have no clue what the fuck you're talking about. I don't have Luna."

"Seriously, Zoo!"

"Ramsey, name a time when I'm not being serious. What the fuck is going on?"

"No, no, no!" I let out a gut-wrenching scream. For once, I was hoping Zoo was being a pain in my ass and had Luna.

"Ramsey, answer me right now. What the fuck is going on? Where the fuck is my daughter?" Zoo yelled. I could tell by his tone he was panicking.

"Zoo, someone took her. I thought it was you. Someone took my baby." I felt like someone was ripping my heart right out of my chest. I could hear shit being tossed around on Zoo's end, while he yelled, flipping out.

"Sis, what's going on?" Zoe's voice came through the phone.

"I don't know. I have to get to the waterfront park," I cried, hanging up the phone.

"Come on, I'll drive," Rory announced.

～

PULLING UP TO THE PARK, I barely let Rory stop the car before I hopped out, running full speed through the parking lot. I didn't have a problem finding the scene because I could see the police observing the crime scene, and Zoo raising hell.

"Don't tell me to calm down. What you need to be doing is talking to that bitch so you can figure out where the fuck my daughter is." Zoo spazzed out on the police officer.

"He's right. Where the fuck is my daughter?" I yelled, running up on Jen.

"Ramsey, listen, it's not her fault," Lance added. His presence caught me off guard. He was the last person I expected to see standing by Jen's side, protecting and consoling her. I was shocked to see him standing there period.

"What the fuck are you doing here? What did you do with my baby, Lance? It was probably you who had someone take her."

Seeing him around pissed me off, causing me to take all my anger and frustration out on him. I rained blows against his chest while I screamed insults in his face.

"That isn't his fault either," Jen yelled, shoving me away from him roughly. I was about to pop off on her ass until I felt Zoe pull me back.

"I understand everyone is upset, but I need to ask everyone to calm down," the white officer yelled over our chaos.

"What the fuck are you resting your hand on your belt for?" Zoo yelled in the officer's face. "I know you're not reaching for your gun."

"Everyone, please, just relax," another officer, who was black, spoke.

"I'm not doing shit when my daughter is missing, and your fellow pig mate is reaching for his gun while speaking to my fucking girl!" Zoo spazzed out.

"Sir, no need to be disrespectful." The black officer tried to deflate the escalating altercation.

"Sir, I thought you were the child's father?" The white officer ignored Zoo, addressing Lance.

"Don't use the word father too loosely with him. He's just the sorry piece of shit who helped my sister create my niece and nephew, and that's about all he has done," Rory spoke. If looks could kill, the police would be zipping Lance up in a body bag.

"He's a nobody. Please don't even address him; he doesn't have the right. I don't even know why he's here."

"Fuck all that, somebody needs to tell me what's going on with my daughter," Zoo yelled.

"May I speak with you over here?" the detective asked Zoo and me.

Stepping away from Jen and Lance's sorry ass, Zoo, Zoe, Rory and I gave the detective our undivided attention.

"Sir, by the statement we gathered for Ms. Garnet and her boyfriend—"

"Boyfriend?" I asked, cutting the detective off, looking from Jennifer to Lance.

"Chill, baby, we'll address all that extra shit later. Right now, fuck them. Their relationship at the moment is not important." Zoo stopped me from going off.

He was right, but that didn't stop me from feeling some type of way. I was still ready to take off on their ass.

Clearing his throat, the detective proceeded to read off Jennifer and Lance's statement. "Ms. Garnet said her, her boyfriend and the missing child arrived here at the park around one-thirty, an hour and a half before the child went missing. Ms. Garnet and Mr. Calloway said they were sitting on that bench most of the time while your daughter, Luna, played. Lance admitted he was on his phone most of the time, but looked up often to check on her. He stated that Ms. Garnet had a close eye on Luna the whole time up until she looked down to search throughout her purse for her phone. Ms. Garnet said it took her about three or four minutes to locate her phone, and the moment she looked up to check on Luna, she was gone. I've talked to witnesses, other parents who were out here, letting their kids play at the park, and pretty much each one said nothing or no one seemed out of the ordinary. It sounds like whoever has your daughter knows her. It doesn't sound like they had to struggle with getting Luna to go with them."

"Zouk, she knows better. She knows not to leave with anyone. I just had that talk with her a few weeks ago!" I screamed. I felt like I was living a sick dream. Watching police officers move around and people standing around being nosy, it hit me like a ton of bricks that someone had really taken my baby.

"You stupid bitch. You should've been watching her better!" I charged at Jen. I didn't care about the police being around or me going to jail. "You're too busy parading around with her father to keep a better eye on her. Lance, I'm not surprised about you being a piece of shit. You have the nerve to be out here in the streets, pretending to be a family with my child and have the nerve to allow someone to walk out of the fucking park with her. Y'all better find my daughter before—"

"Ms. Scott, I understand you're upset, but I can't allow you to threaten them."

"Fuck them. My daughter is missing, and we have no clue who took her, and on top of that, I found out my baby sister is sleeping with the deadbeat of my children. You had the nerve to have him around my child like he deserves it," I said, trying to swing on Lance and Jen. Lance had the nerve to block Jen's body with his, preventing my punch from connecting with her face. The nerve of him trying to protect her and not his own daughter from the sick creep who took her.

"Ms. Scott, please calm down. The last thing you want to do is spend your night in the county. If you keep trying to assault them, you will be arrested."

"Arrested? You want to arrest someone? Arrest the sick fuck who took my daughter, or these two bastards. Jen, shut the fuck up! I'm not buying your fake tears. I wouldn't be surprised if you and that nigga had a hand in my daughter's disappearance. Lance, it kills you to know that we chose up, huh!"

"Chose up, huh? Ramsey, please, who do you think you're fooling? From what I heard, that nigga still in love with his baby mama. From my understanding, you and the twins are his fill-in family."

"My nigga, speak on my baby mama or Ramsey again—"

"Sir!" the detective stopped Zoo before he could issue his threat.

"We need to focus on the bigger picture; Luna is missing. Ramsey, fuck Jen and Lance; it's clear they deserve each other." Rory tried to gain control of the situation.

"I need to lie down." It felt like everything was spinning. My heart was hurting, and I felt so lost and powerless. I looked around, and everyone seemed like they were moving around just as lost as me. Jen and Lance were no help, bystanders didn't see anything out of the ordinary, and the police had no leads.

After talking to the detective alone, giving them all of mine and Zoo's information, he told me an Amber Alert would be set in place. I didn't want to leave my baby, but after searching the park ourselves and riding around in the area and coming up with nothing, I made my way home, but not before telling the detective to look at Jen and Lance as their number one suspects. I no longer trusted my sister, and it had everything to do with her switching up over the past year. Lance, I never trusted, and I wouldn't be surprised if he were finally trying to make good on all his empty threats he had made about taking the twins over the years.

RAMSEY

Not knowing where Luna was was driving me crazy. I felt like I was suffocating. I felt paranoid about Luchi being out of my sight. I trusted Zay and knew he would protect Luchi with his life, but I didn't want to chance it, so I picked Luchi up from Zay's on the way home. I needed my baby near me more than ever right now. I didn't know how I would explain to him that his twin was missing.

Pulling up into my driveway, I was happy to see Zoo's car parked beside my car. I was emotional and physically drained, so I was glad to see Zoo here; he could help me talk to Luchi.

"Daddy!" Luchi hopped out the car, excited to see Zoo. The whole ride home, Luchi was so happy, telling me everything he had done with his uncle and cousins.

"What's up, dude?" Zoo asked, swooping Luchi up into his arms.

"Nothing, I've missed you. I thought you said you were coming over Uncle Zay's?"

"I know," Zoo said, carrying Luchi into the house. I guess he was feeling the same way I felt. He wanted Luchi close to him.

"When is Luna coming back home from Jen's?" was the first thing out of Luchi's mouth once we entered the living room. He hated being home without her. I wanted to break down, but I had to keep it together for Luchi. I didn't want to scare him.

I looked from Zoo to Rory for one of them to rescue me. I couldn't bring myself to tell my son someone had kidnapped his sister from the playground.

"Um, so, listen up, dude, we need to talk to you about something." Zoo paused, running his hands over his wavy hair and down his face. He looked so stressed out.

"This can't be good," Luchi said, looking at us with a nervous look on his face.

"It's not." Zoo took a deep breath. I could tell he was trying to find the words to explain to Luchi, but it was challenging for him. "Um, today while Lulu was playing at the park, someone took her."

"What do you mean?" Tears began to form in Luchi's eyes, letting us know he understood exactly what his daddy was saying.

"Lulu is missing. Someone took her, but I promise you we are going to get her back." Zoo hugged him tightly.

Pushing away from Zoo, Luchi took off running upstairs to his room.

"Luchi!" I called out to him, hopping up to chase after him, but I quickly sat back down, feeling light-headed.

"I'll go check on him." Rory raced up the stairs after him.

I allowed the tears I was holding back to fall. "Uggghh!" I let out a much-needed scream.

Standing up, Zoo moved closer to me. Picking me up, Zoo placed me in his lap. Grabbing ahold of my face with both hands, he kissed my lips. It wasn't a sexual kiss; it was a kiss of him reassuring me everything would be okay.

"Let it out. You don't have to be strong; I'll be strong for us," Zoo said, rubbing my back.

I didn't want to be strong, I wanted to fall apart. I felt so incomplete without my daughter. I wanted my daughter back. I didn't want to think about some creep having my baby girl.

I cried in the crook of Zoo's neck as he held me tight.

"I'm going to get her back, baby. I swear to you with my life." Zoo ran his hands through my wild hair.

I cried harder. I truly felt like I was dying. I felt out of control. I needed my daughter—my kids—like I needed air in my lungs to breathe.

"Come on, baby. Let me run you a bath to ease your mind."

"My mind won't be at ease until I have my daughter back, Zoo. What if I don't get her back?" I began to have a panic attack, and it felt like my chest was tightening up.

"Come on, baby, don't talk like that."

"Zoo, I can't breathe." I pulled at the collar of my shirt. I felt like it was choking me.

"Come on, let's go upstairs so you can get out of these clothes." Zoo eased up from the couch, carrying me up the stairs.

"I cleaned up the mess in the bathroom, and I put the thing in the medication cabinet," Rory said, sticking her head out of Luchi's doorway.

"Okay," I said, not really paying her any attention. "Let me down. I want to check on Luchi," I said, trying to wipe my tear-stained face.

"Sister, go get yourself together first. I got him until you do."

"Okay." I let out a frustrated sigh. She was right. Seeing me very upset would only make things worse for Luchi.

Zoo removed my clothes the moment we stepped foot into my room. Taking his hands, Zoo massaged my scalp, something that always calmed me.

"This shit is crazy." Zoo let out a frustrated sigh.

"I wish I could rewind back time. Luna would've stayed home."

Zoo ushered me into the bathroom. I was going through different stages of grief. I went from sad to angry back to sad, then angry again. Now I was blaming myself, wondering how I could've prevented this from happening to my baby.

I felt the vomit moving its way up as I rushed over to the toilet. I didn't want to make a mess again.

"Damn baby, I know it's hard, but you need to calm down. You're making yourself sick."

"I thought I was sick as well, that's why Luna was with Jen. Turns out, I'm pregnant with your baby." The moment I said that, Zoo's eyes traveled down to my belly. "I found out right when Jen called, telling me about Luna," I said, pulling myself up. Going over to the medicine cabinet, I pulled out the positive pregnancy test. "I forgot I was pregnant until now." This isn't how I wanted to tell him he was going to be a father again.

"Damn, for real?" he asked, sounding a little shocked.

"Yep." I said rubbing the baby bump that was already forming.

"Fuck, I want to be happy, but how could I be when our daughter is missing?"

"Zouk, please stop reminding me," I said, stepping into the shower, standing right under the shower head.

Closing my eyes, I cried my heart out. I calmed down a little when I felt Zoo wrap his arms around me.

"I got us, Rah," Zoo whispered over and over again as I cried in his arms. I was falling apart. I wanted, no, needed my baby.

ZOO

After crying for hours, Ramsey finally cried herself to sleep. I stared down at my girl and son as they slept in my arms. Shit broke my heart that my Lulu wasn't there to lay with us. Seeing them sleep peacefully, I could finally allow myself to feel. My emotions from today's events were all over the place. I woke up pissed at the world because of Ramsey and our failing relationship. Shit hadn't been going right since the run-in with Armani. My attitude toward Ramsey changed the day of my family's death anniversary. I was pissed off that Ramsey made that day about her feelings and her feelings alone like she always did, but all that shit went out the window once she told me Luna was missing. Not only was I angry, but I was also afraid. I was once on these streets, so I understood how sick the world could be, and my Lulu was out there alone, instead of at home with her family. Not only was Lulu missing, but the bomb was dropped on me that Ramsey was pregnant with my young one as well. That was the news I had been waiting for, yet the timing was all wrong. I couldn't enjoy the news at all. How could I?

Despite what anyone may think, I loved the twins like they were my own. I was trying my hardest not to go into a dark place about Luna's disappearance like I had with the death of my daughters. I knew the situation would be all bad if both Ramsey and I shut down. My baby was barely holding it together, so I had to be the glue.

Sadly, the same feelings I felt from losing my daughters to the house fire washed over me. As a man who loved, provided and protected his family, there was nothing worse than feeling helpless to a situation. Once again, I felt like I had failed my family.

The police were out doing their job, hopefully, but as Lulu's father, I had to do my job as well to be sure she was brought home safely.

Three years ago, losing my family was my reason to get out of the game. The thought of losing my family again had me ready to jump head first back in. I wanted to leave my wild and unruly ways behind me, but I see people wanted to test me by taking my baby girl.

Y'all know how I feel about Jen, so I won't sugarcoat shit. I wasn't buying that bullshit-ass story she was telling the police. She could do all that whooping and hollering, making it seem like she was all heartbroken about Lulu, but I wasn't buying the shit. The same nosy bitch who always stayed in my and Ramsey's business wanted me to believe she didn't see what happened to my fucking daughter? No, I think she knew exactly what was going on, and her being at the park with Ramsey's shady-ass baby daddy didn't help.

I hadn't been causing chaos on the streets for years, but I still had connections. I had niggas tailing Jen and Lance the moment they pulled out of the park. My gut feeling was telling me they had Lulu, and I wanted them to lead me right to her.

I found shit sick how bad Jen wanted to be Ramsey. I could tell from the jump Jen was jealous of her big sister. She wanted Ramsey's life. The shit was becoming clearer with every passing day. I wasn't surprised about her fucking with Ramsey's weak-ass baby daddy. I could put my money on it that she and his bitch ass had something to do with Lulu being missing.

Feeling Luchi toss and turn, I turned my attention to him. I wanted to fuck the streets up once I saw the tears running down Luchi's face.

"Daddy, I want my sister," he cried out.

"Me too, dude," I said, pulling him close to me.

"I feel like she's okay, but I won't feel better until she's back home." He slightly smiled as tears continued to fall.

"Dude, on my life, I promise to bring her back home where she belongs. I promise I'm going to do better by y'all. I been messing up a lot lately."

"What's the plan?" Luchi asked, sitting up straight.

"Luchi, don't you worry about that, just know I'll handle it."

"You promise?"

"Yeah, I put my life on it, and don't I always come through?"

"Yes, I wish you were my real father," Luchi said, cuddling up to me.

"Luchi, look at me! I am your real father. You're me through and through. I don't want to hear you say that shit again. Let me worry about getting Luna back, and you worry about all the fun shit we're going to do when I do."

"Okay." He gave me a bright smile, letting me know he hung on to my every word.

"Get some rest, my dude."

"Okay, I love you, daddy."

"I love you too."

Laying back on my chest, Luchi rubbed a sleeping Ramsey's cheek. Leaning forward, he kissed her before closing his eyes. It took him a while, but eventually, he fell back asleep.

The more I watched them sleep, the angrier I got. I couldn't even enjoy the fact that I was about to be a father again. Ramsey was lying in my arms, looking beautiful. Although her eyes were puffy from crying so much, and her face was ashy, I saw her glow through it all. She was carrying the life we had created. Kissing Ramsey's lips, I gently slid her on the pillow next to me, trying not to wake her. Kissing Luchi's forehead, I placed him next to her before easing out of bed. I checked on Rory in Luna's room before slipping into the night. The streets were about to be reintroduced to Zoo the fucking animal.

JENNIFER

"Damn Jen, watch out," Lance yelled as I popped up in bed, awakening him from his sleep by hitting him with my wild arms. Just seconds before, I was enjoying a peaceful sleep next to him, then out of nowhere, my body was signaling my brain to get up because something was wrong.

"I'm sorry, baby. I can't sleep; something isn't right. I feel it."

"You right about that. You must've felt the grim reaper creeping through your hallway." Zoo flicked the light on in my bedroom, revealing himself, Zay and Zoe, scaring the shit out of me.

"You sorry motherfuckers are really in here getting a good night's rest. No care in the world, huh?" Zoo let out a menacing laugh. "Wake your bitch ass up," Zoo yelled, hitting Lance with the butt of his gun that I had just realized was in his hand.

Lance quickly popped up, screaming out in pain because of the force Zoo had put behind his licks, splitting Lance's eyebrow in two. Most of the time, Zoo's attitude didn't move me, but tonight, I felt like I was looking in the eyes of the devil himself, and I could admit I was scared for my life. Even the look in Zoe's eyes gave me chills.

"Shut your pussy ass up before I do us all a favor and take your useless ass out of your misery. I want you sorry motherfuckers to sit straight up and put your hands where I can see them," Zoo announced, waving his gun around at Lance and me. If I didn't think so before, I now knew for sure that this nigga was real deal crazy.

"Now, we're going to try this shit again, and I don't want you to leave not one fucking detail out. Someone is testing me, but what they didn't realize is that they pulled the wrong fucking card by touching my daughter. I want my fucking daughter back, and if I have to make the state of Kentucky bleed, so fucking be it. With that being said, which one of you wants to go first replaying the events of your day? I want a fucking play by play."

"Man, we weren't lying at the park. We told the police everything that happened." Lance was the first to speak. For the first time in a long time, I couldn't find my voice. It was something in the tone of Zoo's voice, and the darkness in his eyes that let me know my smart antics that I normally tried on him would land me in the grave if I tried that shit tonight. I could tell Zoo was itching to pull the trigger.

"I want you to tell me everything, and if I even feel like there's something off a little bit about your story, I won't hesitate to body you both, and you can spend eternity in hell together, talking about how you wish you never thought to cross me and my girl."

"Jen, please don't try to call my fucking bluff, thinking just because you're Ramsey's baby sister it will spare your ass because it won't. Although Ramsey knows your nothing-ass ain't shit but a sorry, hating-ass bitch who's jealous of her, for some reason, she still loves your ass. I know me killing you would end my relationship with my girl, but for my daughter, that's something I'm willing to risk. Just so you don't think I'm bullshitting, I want you to go first, and let some shit not make sense; I promise I'll make you and this bitch a distant memory. Now start talking."

I wanted to tell Zoo the same story I had told the police, but I wasn't ready to die tonight. Taking a deep breath, I began to speak.

"I had planned a family day for me, Lance and Luna."

"Pause." Zoo stopped me from speaking. "First and final warning, from this moment forward, choose your words wisely," Zoo said, pointing the gun at me.

"Um...okay," I spoke nervously. "Ramsey asked me to watch Luna because she hadn't been feeling well. Luna was tired of hanging around the house and asked could we go to the park, so Lance and I took her to the waterfront. My car was parked right there across the park, so I allowed Luna to run off to play while I stayed in the car. I had a perfect view of the park. Luna spent most of her time on the swing, so she was only a couple feet away from me."

"If my daughter was only a few feet away, and you had so much of a perfect fucking view, how was it possible for a motherfucker to take her?" Zoo asked. The tone of his voice let me know he was running on little to no patience with me.

"Wait one minute, Zoo, now you pause, and from this moment forward, you choose your words wisely," Lance spoke. "You keep screaming about your daughter when it's my blood running through her veins," Lance smirked. I could tell he was trying to torment Zoo but now wasn't the time. I wasn't ready to die.

I was terrified for Lance when Zoo leaped across the bed. I screamed as I watched Zoo do damage to Lance's face with his bare hands.

"You're acting like you're so fucking proud of your blood running through Luna's veins, yet you didn't care enough to protect her!" Zoo yelled as he rained blow after blow to Lance's face.

"Please stop!" I cried out with Lance. I felt his pain.

"Who has my fucking daughter?" Zoo jacked me up by my nightie. I was now afraid that this was the end for me.

"I don't know, I swear! I love my niece. I promise I would never do anything to hurt her. Please let me call for help; he needs a doctor." I cried as I watched Lance fall in and out of consciousness.

"Do you honestly think I give a fuck if this nigga lives or dies? He could be the first motherfucker who dies in my city-wide murder spree, and bitch, you can be second. You had my daughter's life in your hands, and you played with it!" Zoo screamed in my face. "So, now, I want to play the grim reaper and watch this nigga's soul seep from his body. Bitch, you're really over here hyperventilating over this nigga. I wish you cared as much about my daughter as you do this nigga, maybe she wouldn't be fucking missing!" Zoo yelled in my face. The wild look in his eyes and the way his jaws clenched had me doing something I hadn't done in a while. I said a silent prayer.

"Zoo, please."

"Your pleas don't mean shit to me, but I'll let you live for now. Bitch, you better not get an ounce of sleep until my daughter comes home safe. I don't give a fuck if you have to put together your own personal search party. Bitch, you better find my fucking daughter," he said, roughly shoving me back, causing me to hit my head roughly on the headboard.

"Okay!"

"Your life is on the line," Zoo threatened before exiting my room with his brothers. The moment I felt like they were gone, I leaped into action, trying to help Lance. "Hang on, baby. I'm going to get you some help," I cried as I grabbed my phone off the nightstand.

"Nine-one-one, what's your emergency?" the dispatch officer answered.

"Please send help! Someone broke into my house and beat my boyfriend half to death. Please send an ambulance," I yelled into the phone.

"What is your name, ma'am?"

"Jennifer Garnet. My boyfriend's name is Lance Calloway." After giving my address, I tried to console Lance. "I'm here, baby. Please hold on for me. I need you." I cradled him in my arms. I tried not to panic, but that was difficult, seeing that there was blood everywhere.

"I swear I fucking hate Zoo," I cried out. "I hate Ramsey even more because she bought this asshole into our life."

"I love you, Lance. Hang on for me, please." Lance was passed out, and I didn't know if he was okay or not.

I should've known Zoo's crazy ass would be paying me a visit, I just didn't think he would cause this much damage, but who was I kidding? He didn't play any games about my sister and the twins. I know what you're thinking because it's no surprise that most of you don't like me, but I swear I had nothing to do with Luna being taken. Despite my rude attitude and smart mouth, if I didn't care about anything in this world, I truly cared about my niece and nephew. Did I take the blame for Luna getting taken? I truly did. I knew that loving Lance clouded my judgment, and that was one of the reasons I had an underlining beef with Ramsey. For the first time in eight years, I felt bad for loving Lance. Being so into him allowed room for someone to snatch Luna from right under my nose. Sadly, I was glad when Zoo leaped across my bed and started beating Lance's ass. I know it sounds bad, but let me explain why. If their disagreement never would've interrupted my story, I would've had to tell Zoo I was sucking Lance's dick at the time Luna was taken. If I would have admitted that to Zoo, my face would be looking like Lance's, or worse right about now.

I rushed down the stairs to my front door. I knew by the constant banging it had to be the police and paramedics.

"He's upstairs. Come on, follow me this way," I called out to the paramedics in a panic. The moment I unlocked the door, I made my way back upstairs, hoping they would follow. I didn't want to leave Lance alone for too long.

"We have a pulse," the paramedic announced.

"Thank God," I sighed, relieved.

"Let's get him to the hospital."

While they loaded Lance onto a stretcher, I stayed behind to get dressed. Throwing some jean shorts and a t-shirt on, I grabbed my purse and keys. I made it outside just in time. The fact that they were going to pull off without notifying me pissed me off. Hopping in my car, I followed the ambulance to the hospital.

I was in the waiting room, extremely tired, but every time I thought about dozing off, Zoo's words popped up in my head.

"Hello, ma'am, I would like to talk to you regarding Lance Calloway." An older white guy dressed in a suit approached me.

"Yes, how's he doing?" I quickly stood to my feet.

"The doctor will be in shortly to talk to you. I'm Detective Jameson, and I was told you and Mr. Calloway were involved in a home invasion?"

"Yes."

"Can you tell me anything about your attackers?"

What I was about to do went against everything I believed in, but sometimes, you had to go against the code. I was willing to snitch to get Zoo out of my life, that's how much I hated him. "My boyfriend was attacked by three brothers Zouk, Za'Cari and Zoran Taylor. Today, my stepdaughter was taken from the park, and everyone's emotions were at an all-time high. My boyfriend believes Zoo had something to do with her disappearance. We could tell Zoo was upset about Lance accusing him of having something to do with my step-daughter being taken, but we never would've thought he would break into our house and cause us harm. If Lance didn't do everything in his power to protect me, I would be lying up in a hospital bed as well," I cried. My story was false, but my tears were real. Zoe and Zay didn't lay a finger on Lance, but I still wanted them to suffer as well. I hated Zoe as much as I hated Zoo. I started to pray that the niggas in jail passed Zoe's pretty ass around, but I didn't want him to enjoy his stay. Images of Lance's battered face kept popping up in my head. I had already been there for two hours with no clue of how he was doing.

I talked to the detectives for about an hour, giving them all the information I had on Zoo and his brothers, including my sister's address. I wouldn't be surprised if she had something to do with Zoo and his brothers showing up at my house. I knew she was jealous of seeing Lance and me together. She probably thought this would break us up, but that wasn't happening. I was going to stay by my man's side, and hopefully, by the time they woke up, the police would be at their doorstep to lock Zoo's crazy ass and his brothers up.

2

ZOO

I got little to no sleep last night. Ramsey woke up this morning, doing little to nothing to keep herself together. She barely got out of bed, and when it came to showering and making her eat, that responsibility was left up to me.

Going into the bedroom we shared, it was dark and gloomy. Opening the curtain, Ramsey quickly moved under the cover like she was a vampire without a daylight ring. Climbing into bed, I pulled Ramsey close to me.

"What do you need from me?" I asked, pulling the cover from over her head. She had tears running down her face. If anything were consistent over the last twenty-four hours, it would be Ramsey's consistent crying.

"You know what I need, Zoo."

"I know, baby, and I'm working on it."

"That's all I need and want, so if you're done bothering me, leave me alone."

Luna being missing had turned Ramsey cold. All she did was cry and snap everyone's head off. Rory and I had been the target of her wrath all morning.

"Luchi and I made you something to eat."

"I'm not hungry, Zouk."

"Ramsey, you need to eat."

"Zouk, what the fuck did I say? Just get out, I'm not hungry! Leave me be!"

"Rah, baby, I'm not about to keep arguing with you about this. I know you're stressed out and worried, shit, we all are, and I don't want to sound insensitive about what you're feeling and going through, but you're carrying a life inside you that needs you to be healthy to grow."

"Zoo, my daughter is missing; I don't give a fuck about eating or you."

"Ramsey, let's not do this." I didn't like this Ramsey. She did and said shit that wasn't in her character. She had no problem doing and saying hurtful shit, thinking that would ease her pain. Sadly, I saw a lot of myself in her. She thought she could mask her pain by covering it up with anger.

"Do what? Zoo, you don't do this! Right now, I can't handle your shit along with all the other shit I have going on."

"When it comes to your health and my unborn, you're going to hear my fucking mouth. All I'm asking you to do is eat something."

"And I'm telling you I don't want to. I don't want to eat, I want my fucking daughter back. Can you give me that instead of giving me some greasy-ass bullshit that's probably going to make my stomach hurt?"

"Fuck, Rah, don't do that!" I yelled. "You don't think I'm trying? Everything you're feeling, I'm feeling the shit, too."

"Try harder, dammit! There's no telling who has our fucking daughter and your main concern right now is me eating some fucking bullshit!"

"Ramsey, don't be her." I let out a frustrated sigh.

"Zoo, I feel like I'm going crazy. Zoo, I need my baby." She broke down. One thing I loved about Ramsey was the way she was always level-headed. Seeing my baby unstable with her emotions, I had to admit, bruised my ego as her man. I felt like I had let her and my kids down.

I held her in my arms until she calmed down.

"Baby, how you feel, I feel as well. I can't eat nor sleep, so I understand everything you're feeling, yet there's a difference between you and me: you have our life growing inside of you. You're the key part of our legacy survival. If you don't eat, our baby don't eat. You can't shut down; Luchi and the baby still need you. Hell, Luna needs you to keep it together. You're giving up, baby, and that ain't you."

I GUESS what I was saying was working. Ramsey tried to pull herself together, but the tears kept flowing; that didn't stop her from quickly wiping them away. "Zoo, I want to be strong, but I can't help that my mind keeps wandering off to the worst possible scenarios. I feel so useless. I want to go out and look for my baby, but where do I start? I have no clue who could've taken her. My money would be on Lance, but I know him too well. Lance never wanted to be a part of the twins' life, he let that be known throughout my whole pregnancy, and his action showed it from the moment they were born. He's too selfish and self-centered, but then again, he knows taking Luna would hurt me. He and Jen would get a sick joy out of seeing me unhappy. Whoever did this is trying to hurt me, and they knew attacking me through my kids would do it." She began to fall apart again.

"BABY, I GOT YOU." I hugged her tight.

"How?" she snapped, pushing me away. "Do you have a fucking lead on Luna's whereabouts?" she screamed, hopping up from the bed as she paced back and forth.

"RAH, I'm trying to be a different Zoo here. I'm trying to be a considerate and patient Zoo, but you're making that very hard for me," I spoke calmly. I could've been controlling and aggressive Zoo, and maybe right now, that's what her ass needed to calm her down. She was flipping every few seconds from sad to mad. Giving it a few more thoughts, I realized it was now time for aggressive Zoo to return. "I know you're hurting, but you're getting too fucking fly with this mouth of yours," I said, gently tapping my index finger against her lips, causing her to smack my hand away. "Stop trying me, Rah. I tried to handle you delicately, but it's clear you're misreading my sympathy for what we're going through with me being some soft-ass nigga. Remember who I really am. I didn't want to handle you, but you insist on making me look like a controlling dick. I get it, and I'm sympathetic to your feelings because mine are identical, but what I can't allow you to do is neglect the needs of your other children. Pull it together. Luchi made you a meal, hoping it will make you feel better, and you're going to eat it for him, yourself and the baby," I said, guiding her into the bathroom. She didn't say anything, but it was clear that her attitude was still there.

All I got from Ramsey was silence. I couldn't believe she was trying to pull a Zoo on Zoo. My family was picking up some of my qualities, and it was all the bad ones. Grabbing a clean rag, I wet it with warm water before washing Ramsey's face. Grabbing the brush, I brushed her wild hair into a ponytail. Wetting her toothbrush, I applied toothpaste before stretching my arm out to hand it to her.

"Are you going to handle your business, or do I need to?"

Looking at me, she rolled her eyes. "Ramsey, grab the fucking toothbrush and stop playing with me."

"No, I can't. The baby doesn't like toothpaste; it makes me sick, causing me to throw up," she whined.

"Well, you and the baby got life fucked up if you think you're about to go nine whole months without brushing your teeth," I said, causing her to laugh.

Grabbing the toothbrush, she whined the whole time she brushed her teeth.

"That's my girl. Meet me downstairs when you're done." I kissed her cheek before leaving out of the bathroom.

RAMSEY

I tossed and turned most of the night, worrying about Luna. I had a feeling this was what slowly dying felt like. My reality was my daughter was missing, and when I fell asleep, I had nightmares Luchi was missing as well. The only thing keeping me from going completely over the edge was when I opened my eyes and saw him lying right next to me.

Around six in the morning, I found it hard to fall back asleep, so I stayed up, worried, watching Luchi sleep. As I watched Luchi, Zoo watched me. Knowing how difficult it was for Zoo to control his attitude, I was proud he hadn't done anything reckless. I was struggling to control my emotions, and I knew I looked like hell because I felt like it. My eyes were puffy, my throat hurt from crying so much, and I knew my hair was a mess because I didn't care to tie it up. I didn't want to fight with Zoo, but I couldn't control my attitude. After handling my hygiene, I made my way downstairs, heading right to the kitchen. I needed to lick some salt to keep myself from throwing up.

Zoo and Luchi were in the living room, watching TV, while I sat in the kitchen with Rory as she made my plate. I still wasn't in the mood to eat, but both Zoo and Rory insisted.

Hearing the doorbell ring, I quickly rushed to get it. I needed to keep myself busy. I was hoping it was someone with information about my baby. I didn't know what to expect once I opened the door, seeing two officers standing there. I felt like the conversation could go two ways: they had found my Lulu safe and unharmed, which I prayed to God would be the outcome, or they had found my baby girl and things weren't looking too good, which I would literally die from heartache.

"Yes, officers, how may I help you? Please tell me you found my baby girl."

The two officers stood before me, looking confused, which scared me into believing they had bad news.

"Is this the residence of Zouk Taylor?" one of the officers spoke up.

"Yes, but no. He's the father of my children."

"Is he here? We would like to speak with him for a moment."

I was confused. This conversation wasn't going the way I expected it to; I thought they were there with news about my daughter.

"One moment, please," I said, trying to close my front door, but one of the officers stopped me.

"It's best you keep the door open."

I didn't like it, but I did what I was told before walking off in search of Zoo.

"Zouk, there are two police officers at the door asking to speak with you."

"What's going on? Do they have some leads on Luna's whereabouts?" he asked, rushing out the living room before he allowed me to answer his questions.

"Zouk Taylor, could you step out so we can talk to you for a moment?" the officer asked once he saw Zoo approaching.

"Yes, tell me you found our daughter safe and unharmed?"

Again, the look of confusion on the officers' faces didn't go unnoticed by me.

"Zouk Taylor, please place your hands behind your back. You're under arrest for breaking and entering and assault with a deadly weapon," one of the officers spoke, removing his handcuff while the other officer held Zoo's hands behind his back. He began to read him his rights.

"What the hell is going on?" I yelled, and the tears began to fall.

"Mama, what's going on?" Luchi asked. He and Rory walked up from behind me. Once he saw Zoo in handcuffs, he lost it. "Daddy, why are they taking you?" Luchi began to scream and cry as well. Running up to Zoo, it broke my heart watching the way Luchi hugged his leg.

"Dude, look at Daddy," Zoo called out to get Luchi's attention. "I know you're hurting, but pick your head up. I got to go, but I'll be back. What I tell you last night? You're me through and through. Dude, I need you to be strong and take care of Mommy like I would." Luchi continued to cry, nodding his head.

"Baby, my phone is on the nightstand. Call my lawyer, Jake Silverman, and he will handle this.

"Rory, please take care of my babies until I return." Zoo spoke to Rory as she held me in her arms as I cried uncontrollably. Yesterday, someone took my daughter, and now today, the police took away my man. I swear when it rains it pours.

I didn't move out of the doorway until the police car pulled away with my love inside. Rushing up the stairs to my bedroom, I quickly snatched Zoo's phone from the nightstand. My fingerprint unlocked his phone as well.

Before I could go through his contact to call his lawyer, Zay's name popped up on the screen.

Answering, I put the call on speakerphone. Just as I was about to speak, Ba'Cari's cries echoed throughout the room.

"Ba'Cari, what's wrong, baby?" I began to panic more.

"Aunt Rah, they're taking my dad." Ba'Cari continued to cry harder.

"Who, sweetie? Who's taking him?" I asked.

"The cops, they're arresting him. I'm scared. Can you have Uncle Zoo come get me?"

"I'm on my way, baby." I grabbed my keys while calling out for Rory.

"I need to go pick up Cari; the police have Zay as well," I cried.

"What the hell is happening right now?" Luchi asked, following behind me as I rushed out the door.

"I'm not leaving until I know my son is straight." I could hear Zay yelling in the background.

"I'm on my way, baby," I reassured Ba'Cari as I backed out of the driveway.

Zay lived about fifteen minutes away. I was so out of it, I didn't understand how we had made it to Zay's house in one piece.

"Cari, are you okay?" I asked, running up to him. The moment my arms wrapped around him, he began to cry again. Three police cars sat outside of Zay's house. The moment the police saw that I had arrived to pick up Cari, the parole car housing Zay pulled away. Cari tried to run after the car, but I stopped him. I hated the fact that Ba'Cari had to see Zay hauled away. All he knew was Zay.

"I'm his aunt; I have him. You can go now! You got what you came here for, now leave!" I yelled, taking my anger and frustration out on the two officers who had stayed behind.

"Come on, Cari, let's get you some clothes and lock up." I ushered him into the house so we could pack him an overnight bag. After packing him a few outfits, Ba'Cari locked up with his door key.

I waited until I got safely into my bedroom before breaking down. I couldn't take it. Not only was Luna missing, but Zoo and Zay were also behind bars, and I had just about the same information on Zoo that I had on my daughter.

Pulling myself together, I called Zoo's lawyer. After I filled him in on the little bit of information I had, he said he would call me back once he knew more.

I had realized with everything going on my nanna was out of the loop. I didn't want to tell her over the phone, so I pulled myself together again so I could pay my grandmother a visit. I had done so much crying in the last twenty-four hours to last a lifetime.

Using her key, Rory let us into Nanna's house.

"My babies!" Nanna cheered as everyone entered her living room. "What's with all the long faces?" Nanna quickly picked up on everyone's mood. "Come give Nanna a hug, fellas," she said, opening her arms wide to them.

Doing as they were told, Cari and Luchi hugged Nanna tight. The moment Nanna wrapped her arms around Cari, he lost it. Shortly after, Luchi broke down as well.

"What is going on?" Nanna asked, concerned.

I wanted to hop on Nanna's lap and cry like a baby as well, but someone needed to be strong for the boys, so I held my tears back.

"Nanna, the last twenty-four hours have been mayhem. Someone took Luna while she was at the park with Jen and Lance yesterday, and the police just showed up to arrest Zoo and Zay," I said, choking back tears.

"What? I'm confused because so many parts of that statement didn't make sense."

"I've been sick lately, so Jen has been keeping Luna because Luchi was with Zay and Cari. What I didn't know before I sent my daughter with Jen was that your granddaughter was dating my children's father."

"That nigga ain't our father," Luchi said, cutting me off.

"Shut up, boy. Right now, that's not important," Nanna fussed.

"From the story Jen told the police, she looked down for a brief second and someone took Luna. Her nor Lance don't have so much as a description of what the person looks like who took Luna. An Amber Alert was issued, but I guess the detectives still have no leads yet. I have no clue what's going on with Zouk and Za'Cari; I'm waiting for the lawyer to call me back." I quickly wiped the tears that fell.

"Father God, I come to You humbly, asking You to protect my granddaughter. I ask for her safe return, Father," Nanna cried out, breaking me down. Nanna's cries were like a chain reaction. I felt so lost. Zoo was the reason I was barely keeping it together, and now he was gone as well. I didn't understand why my family was falling apart. I needed answers, and nobody had any to give me right now.

After Nanna prayed over our family, I waited around Nanna's

house for the call from Zoo's lawyer. I also called the detective on Luna's case. It broke my heart not knowing where my baby was. I didn't know if she was being fed, bathed or being mistreated. The lawyer never called, and it was getting late, so I left to get the boys ready for bed. After getting the boys calm and situated, I asked Rory to keep an eye on the boys before hopping in my car and riding around the city. I couldn't sit in the house feeling like I was doing nothing to get my daughter back.

ZOO

I waited on the other end of the phone for Ramsey to answer. "Baby, you good?" I questioned the moment the phone connected.

"Zoo, please tell me what's going on. I've been waiting for your lawyer to call back, but he never did," Ramsey spoke in a panic. I knew she had to be going crazy right about now because I had given my lawyer instructions not to call her back. I wanted to talk to her first; I needed to feel her out. I had a feeling by the time I got around to calling her, Jen would've run it all in by now, but I guess she didn't because Ramsey wasn't flipping out about it. I didn't want her to know I was locked up for damn near killing her baby daddy and threatening to end her little sister's life. I knew she was already stressed out about Luna being missing and me being locked up, so I didn't want to add this to her plate as well. Truth be told, I didn't know how long I would be locked up. At the time, fucking Lance up seemed like the right thing to do, but right now, a nigga was feeling nothing but regret. Both Za'Cari and Zoran were sitting behind bars, thanks to me. Not only had I taken myself away from my family at the time they needed me the most, but my actions had also taken my brother away from my nephew.

"Ramsey, I don't want you to worry about me, I want you to focus on the kids. Have you heard anything from the detective?" I asked, feeling like shit about being in this situation.

"No, I called, but still nothing," she cried.

"How's Luchi doing?" I asked, thinking about the way he had reacted to the police taking me away. I promised myself at that moment if I got out of this bullshit, I would never get locked up again. I never wanted to see that type of pain in my son's eyes again.

"You know how he and Cari are together, always joking around and up to something, but I could tell them watching you and Zay getting hauled away broke their little spirits. I could barely get Luchi to talk, and when I do, it's something rude. Ba'Cari won't stop crying." I could hear the sadness in her voice.

"You have Ba'Cari?"

"Yeah, he called your phone, wanting you to pick him up because the police were taking Zay. I called your parents to fill them in on what's going on. I gave Cari the option of going with your parents or staying here, and he wanted to stay with Luchi."

"Okay, I love you, Rah."

"I love you too."

"Have you fed my baby?"

"No."

"Come on, get up now while I'm on the phone and make something to eat. Ramsey, I promise if something happens to my baby, I'm telling you right now, I won't forgive you."

"I know, Zoo. I will do better," she whined. I could tell she was doing what I had said because I heard moving around on the other end of the phone. "Zoo, I need you to tell me something."

Letting out a frustrated sigh, I thought about if I should tell her why I was locked up. Our life was already spiraling out of control, and shit could only get worse if I told her what was up. Shit could go left between Ramsey and me, or shit could go left between Jen and Ramsey, and either way, I didn't need this added stress piled on top of everything else my baby was going through.

"Just know I'll be home soon. I love you, Rah. Tell the boys I love them. Take care of yourself and my babies. I'll call you back tomorrow."

"Zoo," she cried.

"I love you. We're going to be okay, Rah! Luna is going to come home safe. We're going to have a healthy baby, and I'll be home and never leave your side again. Believe that."

I hated hearing my girl cry, and the fact that I couldn't be there to hold her had my frustration level through the roof.

"Ramsey, do you want to know why I love you so much?"

"Yes!"

"I love you so much because of your strength, baby! I've always been attracted to your strength and how you always put our kids' needs and wants first, no matter how you're feeling. You need that strength more than ever right now, baby."

"I know, but you're supposed to be here, holding me down, Zoo."

"I know, Rah," I said, feeling like shit. Did I feel bad about beating Lance's ass? No, but I did feel bad about not being there for my family. That nigga was going to get fucked up regardless. I should've moved smarter and waited to end him and that bitch Jen's life after I had my daughter back.

"I love you, Ramsey."

"Love you too." I didn't like the way she said it. I could tell she was losing faith; not just losing faith in me but in life period. I needed out of this motherfucker asap. My family needed me.

3

JEN

Thanks to Zoo being locked up, I didn't have him on my back about looking for Luna, and I could put all my time and focus on being by Lance's side. I called Ramsey every day to stay updated on what was going on. Every day was the same; no such luck. It was like Luna had disappeared. Thanks to Zoo living up to his name and acting like a zoo animal, Lance had been laid up in a hospital bed for a week because he had a skull fracture. Zoo had truly done a number on my baby. If I were only with Lance for his looks, this would be my time to dip out. Lance's face looked terrible, and the bruised tissue around his eyes caused him to look like a raccoon. His lips were now the size of Jay-Z's because of the swelling, and the right side of his forehead was bandaged, covering his stitches. I was so tired of staying in this cold-ass hospital, and I was more than ready to go home with my man.

The first day Lance was hospitalized was the scariest. Things weren't looking well for him at all. His breathing, heart rate, and blood pressure kept dropping, and every thirty minutes, someone was in and out of his room, checking on him.

For the last seven days, my nerves had been shot, thanks to the constant sound of hearing Lance's machines beeping. I missed the sound of my baby's voice. He wasn't in a coma or anything, just in and out of consciousness. Lance would wake up, but when he did, he wasn't up for long. When he was up, he always wore a look of confusion on his face. His eyes were sensitive to light, and his ears were sensitive to noise.

Although I missed hearing his voice and the silence was killing me, knowing he was getting the proper amount of rest to help heal his body relaxed me some. The doctor had him on antibiotics to heal his skull fracture; thank God it wasn't worse than it looked. Although it would take months for him to fully heal, with every passing day, his pain lessened, and that made me happy. It broke my heart to see my baby in so much pain.

"Jennifer, what happened?" Lance's slurred speech grabbed my attention.

"Hello, baby." I smiled, gently kissing his lips.

"What happened?" he asked again.

"You were badly beaten. You've been hospitalized for a skull fracture."

"Get the doctor and tell them to come discharge me. I'm ready to go."

"Baby, slow down. Let the doctor come talk to you first."

"Man, fuck all that. Get someone, so I can get the fuck out of here," Lance yelled, frightening me a little.

Rushing out of his room, I looked around for help. Walking over to the nurse's desk, I grabbed the attention of the nurse sitting behind the desk at the computer.

"Excuse me, my boyfriend is awake now, and he would like to speak with his doctor," I said, pointing in the direction of Lance's hospital room.

"Okay, I'll send someone right in." She politely smiled up at me for a split second before focusing back on the computer.

Walking away, I rushed back to Lance's side. "Baby, the nurse said she's about to send the doctor right in."

"Aye, yo, doc, when can I get the fuck up out of here." Lance rudely spoke to the doctor the moment he walked through the door.

"Mr. Calloway, you were badly beaten—"

"You don't have to fucking remind me, I feel the fucking pain," Lance yelled rudely, cutting the doctor off.

"Mr. Calloway, I'm just trying to explain your condition to help you understand why I would like you to stay in the hospital for a few more days to be monitored."

"I don't have a few more days. I'm not about to lay up in this hospital bed, feeling like a sitting duck. Take all this shit off me so I can get going."

"Lance, just calm down and listen to the doctor."

"How long have I been here?"

"A week."

"A week too fucking long. I'm ready to go, so unhook me from all this shit so I can go. Either release me peacefully, or I will start fucking shit up, and security will need to be called," Lance yelled so loud, causing me and the doctor to jump, frightened.

"Lance, calm down."

"Fuck all that. I want out of this fucking hospital."

"Mr. Calloway, let me explain."

"Motherfucker, did you not hear me?" Lance continued to scream as he pulled the IV from his arm.

"Lance, please calm down."

"Jen, shut up and get my shit!"

"Mr. Calloway, if you're so adamant about leaving, I won't keep you here."

"Good, now, Jen, get my shit!" Lance continued to yell, causing hell. I moved throughout the hospital room, slightly embarrassed by Lance's actions.

I could tell Lance was in pain by the way he slowly got out of bed. I wanted to tell him to stay in the hospital a few more days to allow the doctor to monitor him, yet I didn't want to upset him any further. I was just happy to hear his voice again, although he had done nothing but yell since he had woken up.

I guess the doctor was tired of hearing Lance yell, so he sent a nurse in to discharge him and give him a prescription for the medicine he needed.

~

"I DON'T FEEL comfortable staying here." Lance looked around nervously like Zoo and his brothers were going to pop out of the closet.

"You have nothing to worry about. I handled Zoo."

"What do you mean, you handled Zoo?" he asked, displeased.

Clearing my throat nervously, I spoke. "The police came to question me the night of your attack. I could've lied, but I didn't. I told them who attacked you. Zoo and his brothers are in jail." I smiled nervously. I was proud of taking care of our problem before he was released from the hospital, but by the look on his face, I could tell he wasn't pleased, not one bit.

"Bitch, are you fucking crazy? You did what?" he yelled, wiping the smile off my face.

"Baby, they deserve to be behind bars for what they did to you."

"Bitch, thanks to you being a fucking snitch, our lives are on a fucking countdown. You thought him beating my ass was bad, just imagine what he's going to do once he's released from jail. Bitch, I got to get the fuck out of here!" Lance yelled, quickly getting up out of bed.

"Wait, don't go, I can fix this," I begged, grabbing his arm to stop him from leaving.

"How? You got a large amount of money sitting around somewhere so I can get the fuck out of dodge?"

"No, but I can get it, and we can run away together," I said, trying to hide my excitement. The thought of running away and starting over with Lance made me happy.

"Jen, you better fix this shit, and fast."

"Okay, let's pack, and after we're done, we can go pick up the money and hit the road." I ran to the closet, pulling out three suitcases. Pulling clothes off the hangers, I quickly tossed clothes into the suitcase. I allowed Lance to rest as I packed everything he needed as well.

I knew what I was about to do was fucked up, but I needed to make things right and please my man. I had been doing a lot of fucked up things over the last year, and it was all in the name of love. My feelings for Lance weren't anything new; they had been blossoming and growing over the years. The moment Ramsey brought him around, and I laid eyes on him, I felt the love. My puppy love brought us here, finally together. I got my man by being sneaky and conniving. What Ramsey didn't know was I was the cause of all she and Lance's problems throughout the years. I was the one placing doubt in Lance's head from the beginning.

Back then, Lance used to call me his little spy. Ramsey never knew who was telling Lance all her business, plus starting up lies and rumors, but it was always me. Sometimes I would lie just to start an argument between them. Just imagine how hurt and disappointed I was when I found out Ramsey was pregnant by the man I loved. I knew I was too young, and Lance didn't look at me the way I looked at him, but my young heart still had hope.

Watching my sister carry Lance's babies made me bitter toward her, so I caused major problems in their relationship. I even went as far as telling Lance the twins weren't his, and that was the cause of him walking out of their life when they were two. If I couldn't have him, neither could Ramsey. I didn't feel bad for the twins because they were young enough to forget him. I loved watching Ramsey shut down after Lance left her. Without Lance in the picture, my relationship with Ramsey got better. I loved the twins so much because they were a part of Lance.

Things between Ramsey and I started getting rocky again when Zoo entered the picture. From the moment I laid eyes on him, I knew he would be trouble. I couldn't stand his boss like attitude; he felt like every room he stepped in, he owned. I also hated how he fell all over Ramsey, and he didn't even know her. That was normal; men always thought Ramsey was something special. Ramsey was always everyone's favorite, and that was why I really hated her. Although my mama wasn't a huge part of our life, she always looked out for Ramsey and the twins. Rory never said it, but it was all in her actions. Ramsey was Rory's favorite as well. The same with my nanna, but the differences between she and everyone else was she had no problem telling you Ramsey was her favorite. She would do anything for Ramsey. Now, me, on the other hand, Nanna couldn't care less about me, and that was why I didn't feel bad about what I was about to do.

Lance decided to wait in the car while I let myself inside Nanna's with my key. Nanna was old school; she didn't believe in the bank or allowing someone else to manage her money, so I knew she had money stashed away somewhere throughout her house. My granddaddy was in the military as well, and before he died, he made sure my nanna was straight for the rest of her days. My nanna went over to her neighbors Ms. Jean house every day around this time, so I knew I could look around without getting caught. I knew I had to move quickly because I didn't know when she would return, and I knew the money wouldn't be easy to find.

Starting in the living room, I tossed shit everywhere, coming up empty-handed. Next, I made my way to the twins' room they had at Nanna's and continued to toss shit around. I was making such a mess because I wanted it to seem like a robbery. Despite what I was doing being really fucked up, I really did love my nanna, and I knew this would hurt her knowing this had come from a child she had raised as her own. I had now tossed the whole house around, looking for this money. I just knew it was hidden somewhere in Nanna's room, but she had me fooled. The last room I was about to check was Ramsey's old room. My intuition was telling me the money was inside there, and that pissed me off. Storming into the room, I started breaking shit just because. After kicking over a chair, I backed into the wall, trying to catch my breath. Once I backed into the wall, I knocked the picture of Ramsey over. I watched the picture fall over, and my eyes lit up. I was now staring at a wall safe.

"Bingo! Time to start our new life," I cheered. Walking over to the safe, I checked out the keypad. "What the fuck." I let out a frustrated sigh because I had no clue what her code could be. First, I tried my granddaddy's birthday and their anniversary, but that wasn't it. I tried my birthday, Rory's and the twins, and that didn't work, either. I held my breath as I typed in Ramsey's birthday, and was somewhat relieved and disappointed when it didn't work. I didn't know what else it could be, then a voice in my head told me to try Ramsey's birthday backward. I jumped for joy when it popped open. My eyes lit up when I saw how much was inside. I wasn't trying to clean my nanna out, I just needed enough to get us by, so I grabbed two of the neatly stacked hundreds before shutting the safe back and running out the house, leaving the front door open. Hopping in my car, I quickly drove away.

"Took you long enough. How did shit go?" Lance barked the moment I pushed my foot on the gas pedal.

"Everything went great, so tell me where to?" I looked over at Lance lovingly. I was so excited about running away and starting a life with him. As long as I was with him, I didn't need anybody else. I knew getting Zoo locked up would work in my favor. I didn't think it would play out like this, but I was happy that it had. Hopping on the highway, I drove out of Louisville in search of a new life for Lance and me.

RAMSEY

Stress was all I knew at this point in my life. The last week had been nothing but pure hell. I didn't know how I was getting out of bed every morning. Luna was still missing, and Zoo was still locked up. I couldn't take anything else happening right now. I missed Luna and Zoo so much.

Hearing my phone ring, I was hoping it was the detective calling about Luna, or Zoo calling from jail.

"Hello?" I answered, seeing it was my nanna calling.

"I'm going to kill that little bitch," Nanna yelled into the phone. "That heifer has always been a troubled one, but I never thought she would cross me!"

"Nanna, calm down, what happened?" I asked, concerned when I heard the anger in her voice.

"That damn Jen is what happened! You and Rory need to get over here, now." My nanna began to cry.

"I'm on my way." I hopped up, looking for my shoes.

"Hurry," she cried before hanging up.

"Rory, come on, we need to get to Nanna's. Jen's dumb ass done struck again." I walked into the living room, grabbing my purse and keys off the end table.

"Do I want to know what she has done now?"

"Even if you did want to know, I couldn't tell you because Nanna was flipping out so much, she never got around to telling me what your evil little sister did. She just told me we needed to get to her house asap. Luchi and Cari, come on, we need to make a run!" I called up the stairs to them.

Luchi and Ba'Cari hadn't been themselves since Zoo, Zay and Zoe had gotten arrested. Knowing they were behind bars did something to the boys' spirit. Cari never went more than a few days without seeing his daddy, and it broke my heart listening to him cry every night. I appreciated Crash coming to get the boys out of the house and doing things with them. Since Luna had been missing, Luchi hated leaving my side.

Rushing out the house, we made our way to Nanna's in no time. She was standing on the front porch, pacing back and forth.

"Nanna, what's wrong?" Luchi asked, running to her side.

"Go look at my damn house, it's a mess. I don't know what's gotten into that damn girl. You know what, I take that back; Jen ain't never been right."

Rushing inside to see what had Nanna so upset, I couldn't believe my eyes.

"I saw Jen rushing out of here as I was making my way back from Ms. Jean's house. I didn't think anything of it because you know how Jen is. Her fast ass is forever in a rush, plus I knew she was with that no-good negro. The closer I got to my house, I realized that heifer had left my door wide open! Strike one! I walked inside and saw the mess she had made in every room; my house looked like a hurricane had hit! Strike two! Something told me she was looking for something, and going into your old room, I realized the picture that covered my wall safe was knocked down. That no-good hussy stole money from me, strike fucking three!" Nanna screamed. I could hear the hurt and pain running through her voice.

Pulling out her phone, Rory called Jen. My anger grew as I listened to the phone ring. Rory had the call on speakerphone.

"Hello!" she answered cheerfully as if she hadn't just wronged our nanna.

"Bitch, when I find you, I'm going to beat your ungrateful ass!" Rory threatened.

"Don't call my phone with that, Rory. I haven't done a damn thing to you." Jen played like she didn't know what was going on.

"Bitch, you had the nerve to bite the hand that's been feeding you all your life, so like I said, bitch when I find you, I'm going to beat your ungrateful ass!" Rory yelled to get her point across.

"You can come looking for me, but Lance and I are long gone. My man and I are starting a new life together," Jen spoke proudly.

"Your man? You mean your sister's sorry-ass baby daddy?" Luchi yelled. He was starting to wear his emotions on his sleeve; it was clear he was disgusted by Jen's actions.

"Luchi, you need to stay in a child's place. That's why your father wants nothing to do with you now because of your slick-ass mouth." Jen had the nerve to say to my son.

"Fuck Lance!" Luchi and I yelled at the same time.

"That bitch-ass nigga ain't my father. The greatness of Zouk Taylor runs through my fucking veins. I'm a reflection of the mighty Zoo through and through. Fuck you and that coward." Luchi spat venom Jen's way, and he was right. From his facial expression, from the way he arranged his words to get his point across, it was Zoo through and through.

"Bitch, don't ever say no shit like that to my son again. My kids ain't never needed that nigga in their eight years they walked this earth. That nigga really got your head gone to the point where you would fuck over the only woman who ever gave a fuck to stick around and have your back through right or wrong."

"Nanna isn't going to miss that little money I took. She has more than enough to be tripping off the few thousands." Jen tried to justify her actions.

"Bitch, thousands! You really had the balls to steal thousands of dollars from my granny? Aw, yeah, bitch, your days are numbered!" Rory yelled, now pacing back and forth.

"Jen, if you don't bring my money back, I'm going to hunt your ass down and kill you myself. I don't give a damn if I was a millionaire, it wasn't your money to take," Nanna said, finally speaking.

"I'm sorry, Nanna, I can't. I had no choice. I needed the money fast, and you were the only person I could think of. We wouldn't have to run if Ramsey never would've brought that crazy motherfucker into our lives."

"All your life you've blamed others for your actions, Jen. Ramsey or Zoo didn't make you steal from me; you did that shit on your own," Nanna yelled.

"Nanna, I didn't want to, but I had no choice. Lance and I needed to get out of town to get away from that animal Ramsey calls a man."

"I should've known this had everything to do with Lance. His coward ass has always been a runner when shit gets hard so I wouldn't be surprised if this was his idea." I let out a sarcastic laugh.

"Girl, please, we decided to leave town because we wanted to start over together with no baggage in the way." I could tell she had said that just to bother me, but little did she know, I couldn't care less about her and Lance skipping town to live what they thought was a happily ever after. All I wanted was my daughter and the father of my children. Then, something hit me. What if they were leaving town with my Luna with them?

Beginning to panic, it dawned on me they could be skipping town with my daughter.

"Jen, I swear if you have my daughter with you, I will kill you and that nigga!" I yelled.

"Bitch, I said we were leaving town to start over with no baggage. I don't have your daughter, and if I'm being honest, I really don't care who does. All I care about is my new life with my man. I'm driving, so I have to go." Jen hung up before I could say anything else.

I tried to call back several times, receiving no answer. Breaking down, I lost it, wondering if Lance and Jen were leaving town with my daughter.

Calling the detective on Luna's case, I told him Jen and Lance were skipping town, and I suspected they had Luna. He wasted no time issuing another Amber Alert with Jen and Lance's information and description. If they did have Luna, they weren't getting very far.

I had been on pins and needles for hours, waiting for that call to hear about if they had found my Luna. The moment I got the call, I risked running stop signs and red lights to get my baby.

I rushed throughout the children's hospital, following the directions the lady at the information desk gave me to get to Luna's hospital room. Luchi, Rory, Nanna, and Cari were a few steps behind me. I was so excited about them finding my baby, yet I didn't know what to expect when it came to her mental and physical appearance. I guess the Amber Alert put out for Lance, Jen and Luna had worked. I didn't have many details, and right now, I didn't care; I just wanted to see and hold my daughter in my arms.

I spotted the two detectives on Luna's case standing near her door. "Where is my daughter?" I asked out of breath.

"This way," Detective Palms said while holding the door open for us to enter.

"Lulu!" I screamed once I laid eyes on her. Tears of joys slid down my cheeks.

"Hey, mama!" Her bright smile lit up my world. I didn't know if she was hurt or not, but I couldn't resist hugging her tight.

"I've missed you, Lulu." I kissed all over her face.

"I've missed you all, too. Aunt Nicki was fun, but I was ready to come home," she explained.

"Nicki?" Rory and I spoke at the same time, turning in Detective Palms' direction. I had a feeling where this was going.

"Luna, Aunt Rory and I are going to step outside the door for a few seconds, but I promise I won't be too far," I said to reassure her, but more so myself.

"Okay, come here, big heads," she called out to Luchi and Cari.

"Detective Palms, may I speak to you for a moment?" I said so he and his partner could follow us out into the hallway.

"Yes, Ms. Scott. I was trying to give you a moment with Luna before I filled you in on the case."

"Where did you find my daughter?"

"After issuing the Amber Alert, we received a call about your daughter's whereabouts. Do you know a lady by the name of Nikita Reeds?"

"Yes, she is Lance Calloway's sister, which makes her Luna's aunt," Rory answered for me. I could tell by her tone, Nicki was now on Rory's hit list.

"We found Luna in the custody of Ms. Reeds. As you suspected, Lance Calloway and Jennifer Garett played a part in your daughter's kidnapping. We don't have a motive for why because both Mr. Calloway and Ms. Garett are still claiming their innocence. I would like to talk to Luna, but I wanted to wait for your arrival."

"Okay, that's fine." We all made our way back inside Luna's hospital room. I had to brace myself. I was praying Luna didn't go through anything traumatic while in the care of Nicki.

My heart melted as I watched Luchi and Cari laugh and joke around for the first time in a week.

"Hey, boys, the detective would like to talk to Luna for a second," Rory announced.

Cari moved to the side, yet Luchi moved closer to Luna, protecting her as if the detective said he was going to take Luna away as the detective and I stood next to Luna's hospital bed.

"Hey, Luna, do you mind if I ask you a few questions?"

"No, I don't mind." Luna smiled, causing me to smile as well.

"Do you remember going to the waterfront park last week?"

"Yes, my Aunt Jen and Uncle Lance took me because I was bored sitting around the house."

"Your Uncle Lance?" Detective Palms asked, confused.

"Yes, my Aunt Jen's boyfriend."

Detective Palms looked at me confused. I didn't say anything, I just shook my head. I wasn't surprised that Jen had Lance around Luna against my wishes, nor was I surprised that this bitch and Lance's sorry ass had introduced himself as someone else to Luna.

"Do you remember leaving the waterfront?" Detective Palms asked.

"Yes, Aunt Jen and Uncle Lance said they had a few errands to run, so Aunt Nicki came to pick me up. I didn't mind going with her because Aunt Nicki has a daughter named Aubrey. I was happy to finally play with a girl. I love y'all, but you guys never want to play girl stuff with me," she said to Luchi and Cari.

"Once you were with your Aunt Nicki, did Jennifer Garrett or Lance Calloway visit?"

"No, my Aunt Nicki tried to call my Aunt Jen because I was ready to go home, but she never answered. I gave my Aunt Nicki my mama, daddy, and brother's number, but she said they weren't answering, so I had to stay with her." My blood was boiling knowing that my daughter was asking for us and Nicki was lying to her as if I didn't want her.

"How did your Aunt Nicki treat you?"

"She was nice," Luna spoke nonchalantly. It was clear she didn't know what was going on. I could tell she just thought she was visiting a family member and not being held against her will.

The knock on the door grabbed our attention.

"Hello." An older woman smiled, walking in. "I'm Doctor Jessie. I'm here to check the little lady out." She smiled at Luna. Everyone but me left the room while the doctor examined Luna for abuse.

I held my breath throughout the whole exam. I was afraid to find out if something had happened to my daughter that would scar her for life. I didn't think Lance, Jen or Nicki were capable of harming Luna, but then again, I didn't think they would be crazy enough to take her, so, at this point, anything was possible.

I was relieved to find out everything was fine with Luna and no harm had come to her. From what Luna was telling the doctor when she asked questions, Nicki took good care of her. That still didn't take away the fact that I wanted to rip her head off. I wasn't surprised Nicki had played a huge role in all this. Nicki wasn't a bad person, just dumb, and she felt like her deadbeat-ass brother did no wrong.

"Everything looks great with Luna's health, and she's free to go home," the doctor announced after giving Luna some stickers for doing a good job.

"Thank you." I hugged Luna, kissing her forehead. Moments later, Rory, my nanna and the boys re-entered.

"I'm ready to take my baby home. I'm going to walk out here and thank the detectives and get her discharge papers," I announced, getting up from the bed.

After thanking the detectives and him promising to keep me updated on what would happen to Lance, Nicki and Jen, I walked over to the nurses' desk.

"Excuse me, Ramsey," someone called out from behind me.

"Yes?" I turned around to see a woman standing there with a little boy. When I looked into the little boy's face, I was taken aback by how much he looked like my kids, mainly Luchi.

"My name is Summers, and this is my son, Journee. May I speak to you for a moment?"

"Um, yeah." I stepped away from the nurses' desk.

"Is Luna okay?" she asked. My guard immediately went up at the mention of Luna's name. With everything that had happened over the last week or so, I didn't trust anyone even looking at my kids for more than a few seconds.

"Who are you exactly?" My attitude was visible.

"My name is Summers, and this is my son, Journee."

"Yes, I got that part, what's next?" I asked rudely.

"I just wanted to know if Luna was okay." I could tell she was nervous, but I didn't care because I felt she was speaking in a circle. I got her name and the concern she had for Luna, but what I didn't understand was why she was speaking to me about my child when I didn't know her, but by the looks of her son, I had a feeling I knew why.

"I don't want to answer that question without knowing how you know my child."

"Can we sit?"

I wanted to get back to Luna, but it seemed like she needed to get whatever it was off her chest. Taking a seat, I gave Summers my undivided attention.

"I've been here for hours waiting for an update. I saw when you arrived, and I wanted to approach you, but I wanted to give you time with Luna before I asked for a moment of your time. I know you're wondering who I am, and as I said before, I'm Summers Banks, and this is my son, Journee Banks. I know you probably put two and two together by the look of my son because he looks just like your children. I'm also Lance's baby mother, and I was the one who called the police, giving them a tip on your daughter's whereabouts.

"About two years ago, I moved to Atlanta for a job opportunity. I moved back home a few days ago, and I've been looking for Lance. Although he's never been a huge part of Journee's life, I thought after two years, he would like to see him. I received the Amber Alert for your daughter, and I said a prayer for her as I was on my way over to Nicki's house. I was having trouble finding Lance, so I was going over to see if she had heard from him. She seemed surprised once she saw us at the door, but I thought nothing of it. I thought maybe she was shocked because she hadn't seen us for a while. I didn't stay long, just long enough for her to tell me she was looking for Lance as well, and long enough to see Luna. I played it cool until I got outside and called the police. I stayed until the police came, and I followed them here. I just wanted to make sure Luna was okay. Lance has always been a jackass, but I didn't know he was doing shit like this." She shook her head; it was clear she felt the same way about Lance as I did.

"Thank you, I really do appreciate what you did. I've been looking for my daughter for a week, and I never thought to look at Nicki as the suspect. Nicki and I weren't the best of friends, but I never would've thought she would do something like this. I have so many questions for you, but I really need to get back to my daughter. May I have your number?"

"Yes, and if it's okay with you, I would like for the kids to meet."

"Yes, I'll give you a call when I get Luna settled," I said as we exchanged numbers.

It seemed like with every passing day, my life was getting crazier and crazier. Shit continued to pop out on me. I didn't know Lance had other kids besides the twins. Was I surprised to find out my kids had a brother? No, because this was the type of man Lance was. He made kids and didn't take care of them, always going as far as acting like they didn't exist. I never once heard Lance mention a son nor heard the street speak of it. Lance couldn't even deny it if he wanted to. Luna, Luchi, and Journee all looked as if they could pass as triplets. Journee and Luchi could most definitely pass as twins. Looking at him, I felt like I was looking at my son. After saying our goodbyes, I went to gather my family so I could finally take my baby home with me where she belonged.

After bathing and washing Luna's hair, we all piled in my bed to watch a movie, while I finished braiding her hair. Now that I had Lulu back, I wished my Zoo was here. Hearing my phone ring on the nightstand, I knew it had to be him calling. Listening to the operator talk, I followed the instruction so I could hear Zoo's voice.

"Here, Lulu, press zero." I smiled, handing Luna the phone after putting it on speaker phone. Doing as she was told, Luna pressed zero.

"What's up, baby?" Zoo spoke the moment the phone connected.

"Hey, daddy!" Luna screamed excitedly.

"Lulu?" I could hear the shock and excitement in Zoo's voice.

"I miss you, daddy. Where are you at?" She had no clue Zoo was locked up. She had just returned home, and I didn't want to focus on anything negative.

"I miss you, too, baby. I promise I'll be home to see you soon."

"What's good, daddy? Are you keeping your head up in the yard?" Luchi joked. I was glad he was getting back to himself.

Zoo chuckled. "What's up, dude? Are you holding shit down for me like I asked?"

"Yeah, a nigga even found Luna and everything," Luchi joked, causing us to laugh.

"Unc, you know he couldn't make things happen without my help," Cari joked as well.

"Glad to hear my young ones is holding it down like I would." Zoo laughed at them. "I love you, Lulu."

"I love you, too, daddy."

"Come on, Lulu. You wanna go watch the movie *Home* in my room?" Luchi asked, shocking me. I knew he had to really miss Luna because he hated that movie with a passion. He knew the joy it brought her, though.

"What happened around here while I was visiting Aunt Nicki? I came back to royal treatment." Luna smiled, sliding out of my bed. The fact that she didn't know what was going on around her bothered me. I knew I had to have a serious talk with Luna sooner than later; nothing about what had happened to her was okay.

I waited until they were safely out earshot before focusing my attention back to my phone call with Zoo. "Hey, baby, what's new?" I asked.

"I should be asking you that."

"Um, let's see. Jen decided to break into Nanna's house, trash it and steal money. Rory and I called to confront her, and we found out she stole the money so she and Lance could run away together. Something told me they had Luna with them, so I called the detective on the case before they could get too far outta town. They didn't have Luna, but Lance's sister did, and get this, Lance's other baby mama, who nobody knew about is the one who found Luna."

"Do I even want to ask any follow-up questions?"

"No! Don't stress about it, let's just be happy Luna's home. We can talk about everything later. Now we can focus on Daddy coming home with us."

"Trust me, I'm about to make shit happen, so I can get home to you and my babies."

Zoo and I talked on the phone until our time was up. Like every night since Zay had been locked up, he would call and talk to Ba'Cari before bed. I was ready for them to come home for the kids' sake, and I prayed it was sooner than later.

4

ZOO

My house was silent as Zay and I entered. It took a few days, but with all the shit going against Lance and Jen, my lawyer was able to get the case tossed out. From the moment we were arrested, we had been claiming our innocence after feeding my lawyer some bullshit story that worked against Jen and Lance. I told them Jen cried assault to cover her own ass for kidnapping my daughter.

It was now four in the morning, but I didn't give a fuck; I was about to wake the whole house up like it was Christmas morning. Checking Luchi's room, I realized it was empty. I heard the TV coming from Luna's room, and the door was slightly cracked. Rory was knocked out, lightly snoring and all.

Making my way to the room I shared with Ramsey, I watched as they slept peacefully. I didn't see how when everyone was going every which way. Zay rushed around to the other side of the bed, picking up Cari. Walking over to Ramsey, I brushed her wild hair out of her face so I could take in her beautiful features. My baby looked tired, but that didn't take away from her beauty. Reaching over Ramsey, I scooped Luna up into my arms, tightly hugging her. "Daddy?" she questioned, unsure, causing me to smile. I guess she thought she was dreaming before dozing back off to sleep.

"Wake up, Daddy's home!" I yelled, causing Zay to laugh because everyone jumped from their sleep, frightened.

I could tell Ramsey wanted to flip out about me yelling, but she was too excited to see me as she and Luchi jumped into my arms. We all went crashing on the bed because I couldn't hold all three of them as they excitedly moved around.

"Aye, Rah, be careful." I quickly got nervous about someone hitting the baby.

Cari was crying in Zay's arms, hugging him tightly. My brother looked like he aged years over the week and a half all because he was stressed about missing Cari, which was understandable.

"Baby, I've missed you!" Ramsey cried, planting juicy kisses on my lips.

"Mama, stop hogging him," Luna whined, trying to push Ramsey away. A nigga was feeling whole again from all the love.

I guess all the excitement woke Rory up because she was now standing in the doorway, smiling.

"I love y'all, too, but which one of you is cooking breakfast? Me and my bro are hungry as hell," I asked, looking from Ramsey to Rory.

"I'll cook, only if Luna helps me. She makes the best pancakes." Rory smiled at Luna.

"Deal. Daddy, this is about to be the best breakfast you and Uncle Zay ever had because I'm going to make it with love. Nanna said cooking with love makes the meal taste better." Luna's smile brightened the room.

"I can't wait to taste it, I'm starving." I smiled, kissing her cheek before Rory and Luna exited the room.

Hopping up from the bed, Ramsey ran into the closet. Moments later, she emerged with three Footlocker bags. "Here's some basketball shorts and a t-shirt so you can shower." Ramsey smiled, handing them to Zay.

"Damn sis, what are you trying to say?" he joked.

"Nothing," she laughed. I missed the sound of my baby's laughter. "I'm happy you're home, I just want you to be comfortable."

"Good looking." He hugged her before walking out the room. Cari was hot on his heels.

"I'm happy you're home, daddy."

"I'm glad to be home. I missed y'all like crazy. I'm about to take a shower; go set the game up so I can bust your ass a few times."

"I don't know about you busting my ass, but okay!" Luchi hopped down from the bed, running out of the room, leaving Ramsey and me alone.

Grabbing my hand, she led me into the bathroom, shutting the door behind me. She stripped me out of my clothes. Hearing her cry, I turned around to face her.

"I've missed you, too!" I leaned down so our lips could connect. Removing her pajamas, I grabbed her hand, helping her into the shower. After turning the water on, I gave Rah my undivided attention.

"Have you been taking care of my baby?" I asked, placing my hand on her stomach. It seemed like it grew overnight.

"Yes!" she smiled, placing her hand on top of mine.

"First thing in the morning, you need to call and make an appointment, so we can check up on him."

"Him?" she questioned with a worried look on her face.

"Yeah! I hope it's a boy." I smiled at the thought.

"Why would you want to torture us with another Luchi? I can't handle raising another Zoo," she pouted.

"You know what, you're right about that. Luchi is enough." I laughed, kissing her lips. I was still hoping the baby was a boy. I knew Luchi and I could be a lot to handle, so hopefully, the new baby would have Rah's chill attitude. "I still need to tell the kids I'm pregnant, but this is the moment I wanted to share with you. I can finally breathe now that you're home."

"Yeah, we need to talk about a few things, but first, I want to spend time with my kids. After that, I want to fuck you, then get some rest," I said, grabbing her body wash so I could wash her up first. We took turns washing each other up before getting out, getting dressed and joining the rest of the family in the living room. Ramsey went to the kitchen to help Rory.

"Are you ready, daddy?" Luchi asked as I sat next to him.

Luna walked in from the kitchen, climbing into my lap as she laid on my chest. I kissed her forehead before grabbing the controller off the table.

Cari wasn't thinking about the game as he talked nonstop, filling Za'Cari in on what he had missed over the last week and a half. Zay held on to his every word; Cari was Zay's whole heart.

"The food is about ready," Rory called from the kitchen.

Pausing the game, I carried Luna into the kitchen. Luchi, Cari, and Zay weren't too far behind.

Rory and Ramsey were already placing plates on the table once we entered the kitchen. Walking over to Ramsey, I passionately kissed her. I was truly happy to be back home with my family. "I love you, Ramsey."

"I love you more." She wrapped her arms around Luna and me. I eased my hand under my oversized shirt Ramsey wore; I guess she wore big clothes to hide her pregnancy. We weren't quite sure how far along Ramsey was, but I was guessing by her size, she was about five or six months pregnant. I wasn't surprised we hadn't peeped that she was pregnant; the last few months had been hell on our relationship. I was stressing about our fucked-up relationship, so I knew it had to take a toll on Ramsey, causing her to miss all the signs.

"I love y'all." I kissed her again.

"Yeah, yeah, yeah, we love you, too, now come on, shit, I'm hungry," Luchi rudely spoke.

"There's no way you want another one of those," Ramsey whispered for my ears only.

"Don't worry, I'm about to start beating his ass." I kissed her again before sitting.

"Y'all should've been beating his ass," Rory laughed, sitting the rest of the food on the table.

"Can we not talk about something that's not going to happen and eat," Luchi dismissed us.

I laughed because he was right. I wasn't about to do shit to him, and neither was Ramsey. "Let's eat."

We enjoyed an early breakfast together before Zay and Cari drove home, the twins retired to Luchi's room, and Rory went to Luna's bedroom.

I held Ramsey in my arms, rubbing her belly. "Let's talk," I spoke, grabbing her attention.

"I missed you. I missed the sound of your voice." Leaning down, our lips connected.

"Ramsey, I don't want you to ever question or second guess my love again. From the first time I laid eyes on you, I knew there was something about you. I watched y'all drive away in that ambulance that day, and I felt something in my heart I hadn't felt in a long time. I felt like I needed you, so I showed up at the hospital. I didn't know what that shit meant, and it scared me, so yeah, sometimes, I found myself backing away, but I've always loved you and the twins. People have been working overtime trying to break us apart from your wack-ass sister and that bum-ass nigga Lance to Amber even Armani, but this shit is God's plan," I said, rubbing my growing baby inside her belly.

"I know you love us, Zouk. I allowed a lot of motherfuckers who didn't mean us well to get in my head when your actions always showed how much you love us. We've had our ups and downs, but I want to move past that."

"We were moving past it if you wanted to or not. I wasn't going anywhere, and neither is your ass. We were pushing through that shit regardless."

"So, tell me why you were locked up."

"I beat that punk-ass nigga Lance's ass and your snitching-ass sister told the police."

"What!" she yelled, quickly raising up.

"Yo, calm the fuck down, that's why I didn't tell your ass. Lay your ass back down."

"Zoo, when the fuck did that happen?"

"The night of the kidnapping. Did you really think I wouldn't do shit?"

"Tell me what happened, Zouk."

"It's in the past, Rah, so let that shit go. I felt like shit wasn't right with their story of what happened to my daughter, so I went to see them. Lance talked himself right into a fucking coma, end of discussion. Now, get naked." I covered her mouth with mine, kissing her passionately, knowing that would take her mind off the topic. I wasn't about to let her get worked up over a situation that was over. It had been a while, and I missed being inside her. Talking about Lance's bitch ass or Jen's snake ass wasn't something I wanted to do. I wanted to fuck my girl and get a decent sleep, and that was what I planned to do as I removed her clothes and mine.

5

RORY

Everything was getting back to normal in Ramsey's household, thanks to Luna being back home with her family like she belonged. I didn't feel right moving out of Ramsey's with all the madness going on, so I postponed moving out until my niece and Zoo returned.

My realtor never stopped looking for me a home, and about three weeks ago, I had a little free time, so I went to check out a few places. The fourth house into the hunt, I found my perfect, three bedrooms, two baths, and a finished basement. The moment I signed my name on the dotted line, I wasted no time picking out furniture for my new home.

Today was move-in day, and everything was set to arrive at any moment. I stood around, admiring my empty home. I was so happy to be back home in Louisville with my family.

Being away from home for years had me feeling lonely, lost and confused. I felt like my life had no real purpose. I wanted to truly mean something to someone. I wanted someone who felt like they couldn't live without me and a good man nowadays was hard to come by. I wanted unconditional, pure love, and I wanted a baby.

My plan to have a baby sounded perfect in my head. I was more than capable of raising a child on my own, seeing that I was financially capable, I just needed his sperm; I really didn't want any attachments to him. I didn't even plan to tell my potential baby daddy I was pregnant. My plan was to get pregnant by a one-night stand and live happily ever after. I was smart, yet so dumb, and sadly, the damage was already done.

My desperation to feel loved had me doing dumb shit. The moment I laid eyes on Boss, I knew he was "the one". Not the one as in the man I wanted to spend the rest of my life with, but the one as in the one I was going to trap.

I know what I'm saying may sound awful, but I wasn't asking Boss for anything but his sperm. I know what you're thinking, *"You barely even know him."* Health-wise this was a big fucking no-no, but my judgment was clouded by my urge to ease my loneliness. I felt so lonely while I was overseas. Don't get me wrong, I knew my family loved me, but their life continued to move on with or without me. Sometimes I felt like they looked at me as out of sight, out of mind. I wanted the love I witness between my sister and the twins, and now I had it.

That's right, I'm pregnant with a man's child, who I barely even know, and I won't lie, I'm excited about it. I was going on two months, and I had no plans of telling Boss he was the father. If it were up to me, I would pretend like our night after the club never happened. Knowing how niggas worked, I knew he probably didn't want the baby or care anyways.

Rubbing my nonexistent baby bump, I thought about the night my baby was conceived.

When I saw my sister sitting in the corner, talking to some guy, I had to know who he was. I didn't mean to cut their conversation short, but then again, I did. I had to introduce myself to the man sitting before me. I knew I could come off a little strong sometimes, but I had a feeling this time, it would work in my favor. This man was perfect. I quickly fell in love with his milk chocolate skin, thick lips and full beard. I didn't know what was up with them in these nose piercings, but Boss had a hoop nose ring like Zay. I could tell he had a nice body because his muscles damn near ripped through his shirt.

"Hi, I'm Ramsey's sister, Rory," I said, introducing myself.

"What's good? I'm Boss," he said. I could tell by the way his eyes roamed up and down my body, he was checking me out and liked what he saw.

"Nice to meet you, Boss. Do you mind if I sit right here?" I asked, boldly placing myself on his lap before he had a chance to give me permission. I had already had one too many drinks, so I wasn't surprised when I took my boldness one step further by moving my body to the beat of the music. Boss was a sexy chocolate king, but everything that glitter wasn't gold. Pulling my cell phone out of my clutch, I sent Ramsey a text. I was hoping Boss wasn't one of those fine, yet corny-ass niggas. If I weren't already sitting on his dick and couldn't feel his imprint, I would've thought he was one of those little dick, steroid taking ass niggas by the way muscles rippled throughout his body.

"Is dude a cornball?" I texted Ramsey to get her thoughts on this guy, who I had plans on making mine for just tonight.

She began to giggle as she read my text. Feeling my phone vibrate, I checked her message.

From Ramsey: Don't you think you should've asked that before you hopped in the man's lap? Lol

"Cornball?" Boss questioned as he looked over my shoulder, reading my text. "I'm a boss baby, hence the name."

"Damn, who told you to read my shit?" I questioned, closing out of my text message app.

"I didn't need permission, like you felt you didn't need any permission to sit your ass in my lap, now hand me a beer," he demanded. I liked the authority in his tone. I thought I was the bitch in charge, and he had no problem telling me he was that nigga. Doing as I was told, I reached into the ice bucket to grab him a beer.

Jen knew how I worked, so I didn't know why she acted so surprised to see me sitting on Boss' lap. Winking my eye at her, I danced around in his lap. Looking back at him, he sipped his beer with lust-filled eyes.

Ramsey couldn't handle watching women being all over Zoo, so she *excused herself. I wanted to follow, but I couldn't pull myself away from Boss. His muscular hands felt good running up against my thighs as he rapped along with the music in my ear as I moved my body to the beat. I was feeling his vibe so much when the club let out, I wanted to go home with him.*

"I would say that I don't mean to be so forward, but I do. I've been over in South Korea for a while now, and my battery-operated toys stopped doing it for me a long time ago. I'm trying to leave with you and go back to a room. Are you in or are you in?" I showed off my beautiful smile, leaving Boss no other option but to leave with me. Closed mouths didn't get fed, and I was trying to get fed dick all night long.

"How about your sexy ass lead the way," Boss smiled. "That's me over there," he said, pointing to the black Audi parked close by.

"Don't wait up, my baby." I turned to wink at a cheesing Ramsey.

"Where are you going?" Jen popped up. She wanted to ask questions, and I was ready to go.

"Hopefully to get fucked really well," I answered with no shame in my game. It had been a while, and I wasn't trying to wait around a minute longer, entertaining my sisters.

"Not hopefully, that shit's a definite. It's a hopefully you see them tomorrow, now let's go." Boss slapped my ass roughly, causing me to giggle. I loved how his strong hands gripped my ass.

"Well, hopefully, I'll see you in a few days instead of tomorrow. I feel like a nigga fresh out of the joint, finally about to get mine," I cheered.

"Goodnight, crazy, love you!" Ramsey laughed, shaking her head.

"Love you, too, sister. I'll text you my location."

"Okay, goodnight, brother," Ramsey said.

"Night, Rah," Boss spoke before grabbing my hand, guiding me to his car.

Popping the lock, Boss opened the passenger door for me, helping me inside. The moment my body hit the seat, I melted into the seat like butter.

"You good?" he asked, kneeling down beside me.

"Yeah." I let out several moans as his tongue, and juicy lips attacked the side of my neck.

"Okay, but I got one rule while in my car."

"What?"

His hand ran under my dress as he continued to attack my neck. My body shivered as his thumb applied pressure on my clit. Boss had me leaking. "No panties. You don't need them anyway," Boss whispered in my ear, sending more chills down my spine. "I bet I been having this pussy running like a faucet since you laid eyes on me, haven't I?

"Sexy with a big dick, what do you think? Let's just pray you got a big dick and know how to use it," I moaned. Boss now had my thong off, playing inside my wetness.

"Has anyone ever told you your mouth is going to get you in trouble?" Boss smirked.

"I came out my mama's womb a fucking problem, so I've heard that my whole life. I talk my shit because I can back it up."

"Keep that same spirit, you're going to need it," he said, reclining my seat back a little before shutting the door and walking around to the driver's side, hopping in.

He looked over and smiled at me before starting up the car and pulling off. Boss fooled around with the music as he drove. I guess he was trying to set the mood, changing the music from rap to R&B.

"What are you doing?" Boss looked from the road for a split second, smiling at me as I stretched my left leg out on his lap while grabbing his arm, positioning his hand in my lap.

"What's the point in enforcing the no panties rule if you can't have any fun and play a little," I said, moving his hand around, giving him a little encouragement.

"Aye, you wild as fuck," he grinned.

"Listen, being in the military, I follow orders all day long, but sometimes I just like to make my own rules." I laid back, enjoying the feeling of his fingers bringing me pleasure.

"Your shit is wet as fuck. How do you expect me to get us where we're going without crashing? I can't focus on the road, hearing the gushing every time I move my fingers in and out of you." He looked back and forth from the road, watching himself pleasure me. I didn't give a fuck how he got us there as long as he didn't stop. It had been so long since I had felt a man's touch.

"*Figure it out, just don't stop,*" I moaned as I held onto his arm. Quitting was not an option.

My moans filled the car. I was playing a dangerous game with our lives as I held onto his arm for dear life as he quickly moved his fingers in and out of me. Throwing my head back, I screamed out as I came. The way my body was shaking, you could tell it was long overdue.

"*Now, be a good little soldier and follow my orders of sitting back. Let me get us there safe. Are you trying to have a nigga crash? You're sexy as fuck when you're cumming; I got to see that a few more times tonight, and a few more in the morning.*"

I did as I was told, sitting back and relaxing. I was able to get one off, so I was going to be on my best behavior until we got to the room. Okay, who was I kidding? Somehow, my hand found its way into Boss' pants. He told me to sit back and chill, yet he didn't seem to mind. Spitting on my hand, I massaged his dick. I was already in love with his length and size, and I couldn't wait to feel it inside me. My face lit up like a kid in a candy store as I watched him pull up to the hotel.

"*Finish.*" It was Boss' turn now to hold my arm in place as I tried to put his member back in his pants.

"*That was fun and all, but we're here. I want to feel you inside my pussy now, not in my hand.*"

Boss wasted no time giving the valet his key as he jogged around to open the door, helping me out of the car.

"*Your no panties rule is the reason my dress is ruined,*" I pouted. Being in the moment had me walking through this nice hotel with a wet ass.

"*I got you covered,*" Boss smiled, wrapping his arms around me from behind. His lips quickly found my neck.

I stayed wrapped up in Boss' arm while he checked the room out. This was the feeling I missed and craved: to be held and wanted by someone, even if it was just for one night. Something about the way Boss looked at me on the elevator made me nervous. I understood why the moment we walked into the hotel room. I never got the chance to step foot into the hotel room before Boss swept me off my feet, flying through the air. I landed in the middle of the king size bed. "*If you don't want me to rip that dress off you, remove it now.*"

"Do what you gotta do," I challenged.

"You're going to regret saying that. That mouth of yours is going to get you in trouble fucking with me," he said, literally ripping my dress off me. I screamed, shocked and turned on as his muscles flexed. *"First round on you, I'll let you call the shots."*

"First round on me? You're not living up to your name. You're the Boss, but I been handling you since I approached you."

"I tried to give you a chance before I shut this whole show you been performing down, but your mouth..." His index finger tapped my bottom lip. Opening my mouth, I took his finger into my mouth, sucking on it. Smirking, Boss shook his head.

I playfully rolled my eyes. *"Boy!"* I screamed as he pulled me to the edge of the bed.

"Who the fuck are you calling a boy? I'm a fucking Boss, and you're about to find out how I handle my business." He grabbed my face, roughly kissing me. I closed my eyes, enjoying the feeling of his lips and tongue. Grabbing a handful of my hair, he roughly turned me around.

"Oh," I moaned.

"You're good at taking orders, right?" he asked, spreading my legs. I still had my heels on.

"Yes!" I moaned, looking over my shoulder at him.

"Good, I'm going to give you an order, and if you fuck it up, there will be consequences."

"Who do you think you are?" I challenged.

"I am now your boss, and you're now my pretty-ass little soldier. You now take orders from me, understood?"

"Yes."

"While I'm fucking you, if I ask you a question, you now answer me with sir, yes sir, do you understand, my little soldier?" He roughly smacked my ass, causing me to whine.

"Yes, sir."

"Wrong. I said answer me with sir, yes sir." He roughly spanked me twice on the ass.

"Sir, yes sir," I moaned.

"Much better." I could tell by his tone, he was pleased. The combination

of him sucking on my neck and playing in my wetness felt like heaven. "Are you ready for your task?"

"Yes," I answered, and the moment I did, I regretted it. I had forgotten within seconds, thanks to his soft lips being on my neck.

Boss massaged his hand through my scalp before roughly grabbing a handful of my hair. "Wrong again." He roughly smacked my ass again. "I don't want to bruise this pretty ass of yours, so listen, okay?" He pulled my head back. His kiss was so passionate, although he still had a tight grip on my hair.

"Sir, yesssss sir," I moaned out.

"Good." He kissed me again.

"I'm about to eat your pussy. I don't care how good it feels, you better not let them legs give out, understood?"

"Sir, yessss sir," I answered, getting nervous as he dropped down to his knees.

"Um, uh," Boss moaned, flicking his tongue against my clit. "How you're standing when I start is how you should be standing when I finish," Boss announced before burying his face between my legs.

"Wait, Boss, that's not fair," I cried out. I was already feeling the pressure from the buildup, and he wasn't even thirty seconds in. Boss smirked as he looked up at me. Him being so damn sexy didn't help.

It was my turn to pull some hair as I placed both my hands in Boss' fro. Karma was a bitch. I was now looking like the girls I talked about in the club. He had my legs shaking so bad, I now looked like a newborn baby deer just learning to walk. The moment my legs were about to give out on me, Boss quickly hopped to his feet, and in one swift movement, my body was up in the air again, only this time, Boss held me tight in his arms with my legs around his neck while he continued to feast on my pussy. I rode his face until my body felt like lightning bolts had run through it.

"Now, how should you be punished for not listening?" he asked, lying me on the bad.

"I think you had enough spanking." He rolled me over, kissing my ass cheeks. "I think it's time to give that pussy a beating. What position would you like to be fucked in? I think I want to fuck you while you're on a handstand."

"No, Boss, I been drinking. I don't think that will end well."

"What do you mean, no? Rory, you don't have a choice. Didn't I give you the chance to lead and I follow? You allowed your mouth to write you a check your ass can't cash," Boss said, removing his clothes.

Bracing myself, I took a deep breath before doing a front flip and Boss caught my legs. If I knew I would be doing all this tonight during sex, I would've eased up on how many drinks I'd had.

Thank God Boss was strong, and I didn't have to do all the work of holding myself up. "Oh, yes!" I cried out as he eased inside me. My toys held me over, but it was nothing like the real thing.

After we both came in this position, Boss put me in a few more crazy positions, fucking my brains out before we both called it a night. The next morning, I woke up to gentle sex. I guess he could tell I couldn't handle another day of being spanked and rough sex, although I enjoyed it.

That time I spent with Boss was cool for what it was, but he had served his purpose. I was just praying everything worked out like I had planned it.

6

ZA'CARI

Ba'Cari was spending the weekend with Luchi. I guess after following me around and not leaving my side for weeks, he was finally tired of me. On some bored shit, I found myself driving to the river to clear my head and smoke a few blunts. With all the mayhem that had taken place over the last few weeks, with me being locked up, being away from my son and canceling my annual 4th of July celebration, I tried to find peace within this crazy world.

It was a little after one-thirty in the morning in the city, so the waterfront was basically empty, which I was thankful for. It was the summertime, so bad little motherfuckers were normally running around everywhere.

I grabbed my gun before hopping out of my truck. I was no longer into anything crazy. I was well respected in my city, but that never stopped a hating-ass nigga from doing a motherfucker dirty if they felt like you were slipping, so I stayed on my P's and Q's.

I wanted to sit closer to the water, so I made my way through some trees so I could find a bench closer to the river.

I loved summer nights; weather like tonight is what calmed me. I had on a light jacket, but the breeze felt good as fuck. Pulling out my Swisher and weed, I began to roll up.

Nights like these used to be my brothers and I's thing. Sleepless nights we would ride around in silence, looking for spots like this to chill, blazing up to clear our minds. Coming to sit by the water was one of our favorite spots.

Lighting my blunt, I took a long pull, thinking about my son. For the last eight years, it had been just him and me.

Ba'Cari's mama just couldn't get her life together. The same things that attracted me to her were the same things that turned me off about her. Blanca was a hood bitch through and through. When I first met her, that was one of the main reasons I loved her. She was getting more money than most of the niggas I knew, even if it meant bussing a nigga down in a dice game or selling weight. Blanca was also known for having hands. I used to love watching her drag a bitch through the hood, but like I said, the same shit I loved about her was the same shit I hated. The Bonnie and Clyde shit was cute until she got pregnant with Ba'Cari.

Nothing was more embarrassing than watching my seven-month pregnant baby mama stand on the block all day, hustling like she had to. Back then, Zoo and I were into a lot of shit, so I didn't understand why Blanca was going so hard, hustling like a nigga wasn't eating and couldn't take care of her and my seed. Not only was that shit embarrassing, but her fighting never stopped. Blanca was very selfish and didn't give a fuck about anybody but herself. At eight months pregnant, her selfish actions landed her in jail on an attempted murder charge. My son was born while his mother was in jail. I didn't feel like she deserved to be in his life, so she wasn't.

Blanca was charged with first-degree attempted murder, and she was sentenced to thirteen years behind bars. After my son was born, I didn't do much to keep in touch. Ba'Cari was my heart, and Blanca knew that shit from the moment she announced she was pregnant. I didn't understand why she was so careless with her job of carrying him until he graced the world with his presence. It was a blessing that my son had made it into the world without any health issues since Blanca didn't care enough to stop partying and drinking.

I was proud to call Ba'Cari my son. My little man was the smartest kid I knew; he made my stress well worth it.

I was so caught up in thinking about my life, I hadn't noticed someone had been lying on the bench in front of me, balled up in the fetal position, staring directly at me. I could tell by the look on her face she was frightened as her body shivered from the night's breeze.

I intensively stared back at this person, trying to take in all their features with only the dim lights provided by the park. The girl resting before me looked young. She didn't look like she belonged on the streets the way she was dressed. I also noticed the duffle bag she rested her head on.

Checking the time on my watch, I realized it was now almost two-thirty. Standing up, I walked over to her, causing her to quickly raise up on the bench.

"Here!" I said, taking off my jacket. I stopped a couple feet away from her, stretching my arm out with the jacket in my hand. I didn't want her to think I was trying to harm her.

"No!" she said, shaking her head.

"Please!" I said, pushing the jacket toward her.

Relentlessly, she took the jacket from my hand. Backing away, I made my way back over to my seat as I watched her wrap up in my jacket.

I could see her face a little better now that she was sitting up. I could tell she was a baby with no business sleeping in the park this late.

"What are you doing out here so late, lil' mama?" I asked.

Wrapping her arms around her chest, she squeezed herself real tight, I guess to warm herself up as she sat in silence. I understood her unwillingness to talk; she had every right to be standoffish.

"My name is Za'Cari Taylor, what's your name?" I asked, trying a different approach. I didn't miss the look of confusion that crossed her face before she looked away.

I could tell she wanted me to leave her alone, but I couldn't. It was in my nature to help people when I felt it was needed, and something was telling me she was in need of help. I knew she wasn't sleeping in this park this late because she wanted to be.

"I like to come out here to clear my head after a long week or when I'm bored. Normally on Fridays, my son and I stay up all night, playing video games, eating pizza and junk food, but today, he decided to ditch me to spend the weekend with his cousin," I said, making conversation. I saw a faint smile appear on her face.

"My name is Bradleigh," she said a little above a whisper.

"Nice to meet you, Bradleigh," I said before focusing on the river, admiring how the city lit up at night.

"Do you want to answer my original question about what you are doing out here so late?" All she did was shake her head no.

"I know someone is worried about you."

Hopping up, she took my jacket off before throwing the duffle bag over her shoulder.

"Thank you," she said, sitting my jacket beside me before walking off. I wanted to get up and follow behind her, but I didn't want to scare her.

Lighting up another blunt, I sat there trying to figure out her story. I could tell she was young and had no business sleeping in a park. As a parent, I didn't understand how her parents could sleep at night, not knowing if their kid was somewhere safe. Taking a few more pulls from my blunt, I was ready to go home and call it a night. Making my way to my truck, I noticed Bradleigh sitting on a different bench.

Walking over to her, I sat next to her, causing her to look my way. "Listen, I'm not trying to hurt you or anything, I just want to make sure you're okay." Looking at her in a better light, thanks to the lights that aligned the street, I noticed something I hadn't noticed before; she was pregnant.

She realized my focus was on her belly and she began to cry. I looked around, checking my surroundings, realizing me sitting here with a crying, pregnant teen wasn't a good look.

"It's late, can I offer you a ride somewhere?" I asked, not knowing why. I knew she would decline, seeing that she barely wanted to tell me her name. Surprisingly, she shook her head yes before getting up, trying to grab her bag.

"I got it," I offered.

"Thank you!" She faintly smiled. Leading the way to my truck, I placed her bag in the backseat before helping her inside.

"Are you hungry?" I asked, starting up my truck after getting in. I had a feeling if she was sleeping in the park, she hadn't eaten, and had to be hungry as well.

"Um..." I could tell she was about to decline my offer to feed her.

"Do you like White Castles?" I asked since there wasn't much open at these hours, and there was a White Castles right down the street from there.

"Yes."

"Okay, are you still cold? Would you like me to turn on the heat?"

"Yes, please," she answered as I reached over to turn the heat on.

After letting the heat warm up a little, I pulled away so we could get her a hot meal to eat.

Pulling into the White Castles' parking lot, I noticed the inside was extremely packed. Making my way around to the drive-thru, I realized that was packed as well.

"I'm fine, you don't have to wait," Bradleigh spoke, grabbing my attention.

"Are you hungry?" I asked.

"Yes," she answered, looking down as she played with her fingernails.

"Well, I'll wait then," I reassured her.

Several times during our fifteen-minute wait, Bradleigh constantly told me to pull off, but I didn't. After getting our food, I pulled over in an empty parking space. I handed her the four cheeseburgers and fries she had ordered. "Thank you."

"No problem, little one." I smiled at her.

We ate in silence while the music softly played in the background. I was high with the munchies, so I murdered my food within minutes.

Looking over at her, I realized she was silently crying as she ate her food.

"What's wrong, Bradleigh?" Looking at me, I could tell she was beyond heartbroken.

"I appreciate the meal."

"No problem."

"When I'm done eating, you can take me back to the park. I got in your car, accepting the ride you offered, knowing I had no place to go," she cried. "I'm seventeen years old and four months pregnant. I'm homeless because my father kicked me out the moment he found out. I have an older sister, but my father forbade her from helping me. She won't let me stay with her because my parents threatened to cut her off. I have no place to go, so that's why I was sleeping in the park."

"Damn," was all I could say, feeling sorry for her.

"I'm ready to go now, I'm done eating. I no longer have an appetite," she said, putting the rest of her food in the bag.

I stared at her as she cried. "I'm not taking you back to sleep in a damn park. What kind of man would I be?" I said, starting my truck up. I was willing to take her home with me before I allowed her to sleep in a park. I know it's crazy of me to take a stranger home with me, but shit like this, I kind of did on the regular. I stayed taking bitches home with me from the club on a late night, so I didn't see the difference in doing the same for a person in need. She's seventeen and pregnant; there was no way in hell I was leaving her to sleep on the streets.

SHE MOVED SLOWLY throughout my house, taking everything in. "I live here with my eight-year-old son, but like I said earlier, he's spending the weekend at his cousin's house. I have a three bedroom, so you'll have your own space." My spare bedroom was for Zoo; he spent a lot of time here when he was dealing with the loss of his family. "Do you need anything from the kitchen before I show you to your room?"

"No, I'm fine."

"Okay, well, follow me," I said, making my way upstairs.

"This is my son's room," I said, turning on the light switch in his room so she could see inside. I was a stranger to her, so I was trying to make her as comfortable in my home as possible. I wanted her to know I didn't have any hidden motives.

She smiled as she looked around Cari's room. "Over there is the bathroom," I said, moving right along, showing her the bathroom that was across the hall from where she would be sleeping. "This is the room you will be sleeping in; my room is down the hall."

"Thank you again. You can sit my bag on the floor right there." Her voice was so soft, it was almost impossible to hear her.

"Is this good?" I asked, making sure she was comfortable with the room.

"It's perfect." She faintly smiled.

"Do you need anything else before I call it a night?"

"Do you have something I could sleep in? All I have is the clothes on my back and I would really like a shower."

Looking at the duffle bag, I grew confused. "What's in the bag?" I asked, pointing to the duffle.

Walking over to the bag, she unzipped it, revealing all the baby items. "I could only pack what I could carry. It was either my things or my baby's, and I refused for it to come into this world without anything," she spoke. She was now crying again.

"Keep your head up, little one, you're going to be okay," I assured her. "I'll get you a pair of my basketball shorts and a T-shirt." Leaving out of the room, I went into my own to grab the things she needed. I was going to need another blunt before the night was over.

BRADLEIGH

After a long, much-needed shower, I laid in the dark room, thinking about the last twenty-four hours of my life. I knew this day was coming, and I knew it would go something like it did. Not only did I get a new car for a surprise graduation gift, but I also received the hugest surprise in the form of a positive pregnancy test. I couldn't believe I had found out I was carrying a life inside of me two days before I walked across the stage to get my high school diploma.

The moment I found out, I knew I had to keep it a secret as long as I could because I knew my parents wouldn't approve.

My father was Bradsher Lambert, a well-respected pastor on the rise. So many big things were happening for my parents over the past year. My father was moving into a deal to have his church sermon televised on national TV. I was proud of him, but his controlling ways were getting worst now that his life was moving in a different direction. My father was very judgmental and felt his family should be perfect. He disapproved with just about everything, and after a while, I started to become rebellious.

At seventeen, I wanted to hang out with friends, go to the movies, attend teen parties, feel like a normal teen; instead, I spent every waking moment at school or at church. Don't get me wrong, I loved the church, but sometimes, I just wanted to do something I enjoyed without my parents making me feel like I was going to hell because I wanted to have friends or enjoy a little male attention. Most of my friends I met at my private school, and they were just as stuck up as my parents; they didn't enjoy a lot of the things I enjoyed. I felt like I didn't fit in with my family, so I started sneaking off, doing my own thing, and that was what landed me in my situation, four months pregnant and homeless.

I missed my room and bed already, and it hadn't even been a full twenty-four hours yet.

My day had started off with me trying to be as normal as possible. I went on with the day my parents had planned out for me, trying my hardest not to let my morning sickness get the best of me. My father was having a back to school giveaway and volunteered my services to help.

The July weather didn't help the fact that I was sweating bullets under my sundress because I wore a waist trainer to hide my growing belly. I know wearing a waist trainer wasn't the greatest or safest idea, but I had no choice if I wanted to keep my secret a secret.

After a long, miserable day of fake smiling and sneaking off to the bathroom to take the waist trainer off to allow my stomach to be free, what I did notice was my mother watching my every move. When she asked me what was wrong, I just told her it was something I had ate and that I wasn't feeling well.

I was thankful my mother had given me permission to leave early. I quickly rushed home, more than ready to come out of this dress and waist trainer. I began to strip out of my clothes the moment I walked through the front door of our residence.

I was hot, sweaty and in need of a serious shower. Rushing into my room, I made a beeline right to my personal bathroom. By the time I had made it inside, I was completely naked.

Looking down at my stomach, I began to cry. At seventeen, I couldn't believe I had landed myself in the messed-up situation. Not only was I stressed about being seventeen and pregnant, but I was also worried about what my extremely religious family would say. There were so many times where I wanted to sit my parents down and tell them what was going on with me, but I couldn't bring myself to do it. I didn't want to let them down. My father had big dreams for my life, and being a teen mom wasn't in his plans.

After washing my hair and body, I stepped out the shower. Grabbing my towel that rested on the towel rack, I wrapped it around me. Walking into my room, I walked over to my full-length mirror to better examine my body. I knew I wouldn't be able to hide my pregnancy much longer, so I had to come up with a plan.

"Bradleigh, how are you feel—" My mother's voice trailed off into the distance, and her eyes grew big the moment she barged into my room. I quickly reached for my towel to cover my body.

"Mother, I can explain!" I instantly began to cry as I wrapped the towel around me.

"Bradsher!" my mother yelled out for my father as tears ran down her face as well.

"What is it, dear?" My father quickly appeared in the doorway. "Bradleigh, cover yourself." My father's voice boomed throughout my room. Rushing into my closet, I quickly threw on a t-shirt and sweatpants.

I couldn't bring myself to look my mother in the eyes, so I exited my closet with my head held down.

"Now, can someone fill me in. What's with the tears?"

"Bradsher, this can't be happening. When could this have happened?" my mother spoke more to herself as she paced back and forth. "Were private schools, big houses, nice cars and a closet full of clothes not enough? You could have anything your heart desires; all we asked you to do is abide by our rules, go to school, be a good Christian woman and attend church, and what do you do? You stand before me, a huge disappointment," my mother yelled.

My heart was broken by the words she spoke. I expected this kind of rage and anger from my father, and that was why it hurt ten times worst coming from my mother. She was always my voice of reason when it came to getting my father to ease up a little.

"Maggie, what has gotten into you? Why are you speaking to her with such a tone?"

"*Bradleigh, why don't you raise your shirt up and show your father what you've been hiding.*"

"*Mother, please.*"

"*Please what, Bradleigh? How dare you. I want to know when this shit happened,*" my mother yelled, shocking both my father and me.

"*Can someone please fill me in on what's going on? Maggie, you know better than to use that type of language!*"

Walking over to me, my mother roughly grabbed me up by my shirt, dragging me over to my father. "*Let's just say we've raised a Jezebel. This floozy has been keeping a secret for, let's say about four months.*" My mother roughly raised my shirt, revealing my growing baby bump to my father.

"*For heaven sake, Bradleigh, are you trying to ruin me!*" my father yelled, causing me to flinch. "*Pack your things and get out, you're no longer welcome here!*"

"*Father, please!*" I cried.

"*I don't want to hear it, Bradleigh. I can't let you ruin what I'm trying to build all because you can't follow the rules I set for you. Since you can't abide by my rules, you can't stay here. Did you ever, for once, stop to think about how this would affect me, my church, my brand? You're such a selfish child,*" my father continued to yell.

I was hurt, but that was quickly replaced by rage. I never wanted to disrespect my parents, but they were huge hypocrites. They loved preaching the word to others but didn't follow the word themselves. If this were a situation with one of the members of their congregation, this wouldn't be how my parents would tell the parents to handle the situation. My father would be preaching forgiveness and understanding, but he was throwing me out in the streets without a second thought.

Tears clouded my vision as I gently pulled away from my mother. Grabbing my phone, I dialed my older sister.

"*Who do you think you're calling? Is it the nigga who knocked you up?*" my mother asked. It was clear she was in rare form; cursing and using the N-word wasn't normally in her vocabulary. She didn't even sound right using profanity.

Ignoring my parents, I listened to the phone ring until I heard my sister's voice come through the other end of the line. "Hello?"

"Shani, they know, do you think you can come get me?"

"Shantell, you knew?" my father yelled. "Bradleigh is cut off. She's no longer a member of this family, and if you choose to help her, Shani, you will be cut off and disowned as well," my father yelled before exiting my room.

"I'm sorry, Brad," Shani said before hanging up. I couldn't believe my family was turning their back on me so easily.

My mother stood there watching my every move. "Since you don't know how you're getting to where you're going, I suggest you pack lightly."

"Be strong, Brad," I whispered to myself. I had to encourage myself to keep from falling apart. I didn't know my next move. I could bet my father was making calls right now to threaten the rest of my family the same way he had threatened Shani. Walking into my closet, I changed out of the sweatpants and shirt I had on. Since my secret was out, I wasn't about to burden myself with wearing extra clothes to cover my bump. Grabbing my pink Nike duffle bag, I threw it over my shoulder.

"I see you're prepared." My mother shook her head. Grabbing my purse, I walked past her with my head held high. "Not so fast. Credit cards and keys." I felt this moment coming, and sadly, I was prepared for it. I played out the different scenarios of how my parents would react to my pregnancy in my head, and it always came back to them either trying to get rid of my baby or me. If they wanted me to get rid of my baby, I was willing to leave on my own because that wasn't an option. Unzipping the inside pocket of my purse, I handed my mother my credit card and keys before leaving the only home I knew.

I had no transportation or destination, so I took off walking. It was daytime, and the city was busy. I had a few hours to get my sleep situation together. My mind was so busy with so many mixed emotions, I hadn't realized I had been walking hours and had made my way to the waterfront. I had been there for hours, and night was falling. I began to cry again because I had no clue what to do next. It killed me because it looked like I would be sleeping in the park, and then Zay showed up.

Hearing the door crack, I quickly rose. "Yes?" I asked Zay.

"I was just checking on you. Do you need anything?"

"No, thank you, I'm fine."

"Well, I bought you a bottle of water and a pop just in case you got thirsty. May I come in?" he asked.

"Yeah, of course," I said, sitting all the way up in the bed.

Walking in, Zay sat the bottle of water and can of pop on the nightstand.

"Thank you."

"How is the temperature in here? Are you hot, cold?"

"No, I'm fine. Really, Zay, thanks for everything. You didn't have to help me, but you did."

"No problem. A park is no place for a little girl to sleep." He smiled, and I frowned. Did he see this growing belly? I was far from a little girl.

"Goodnight." I tried to control my attitude.

"Damn, are you putting me out?" he chuckled. "Goodnight, Brad," he said, walking off.

"Zay?" I called out.

"Yeah?" He turned back around to face me.

"Can you turn the light out for me?"

"Sure, lil' mama." He showed off his handsome smile.

I was grateful for Zay taking me in, but I knew this was only temporary, causing another layer of stress to wash over me. I planned to hide away. Hopefully, if I stayed out of sight, Zay would forget about me, giving me enough time to come up with my next step in life.

ZAY

It was now Sunday night, and Bradleigh had barely come out of the room. When she did, she did a lot of sneaking around like she was afraid of me. I would cook her three meals a day, and she would refuse to come out to eat with me. She would wait until I made a run, or she would wait until I went to sleep to eat. I knew all the shit she was going through had her stressed out, so I decided to give her some space to get her mind right.

"Dad, where are you?" Ba'Cari yelled as I heard the front door open and close. I was confused on what he was doing here. My brother or Rah hadn't called me, telling me they were on their way. Getting up from the couch, I met him halfway through the house.

"What's up, son? How did you get here?" I asked, looking to see if my brother or Rah were behind him.

"I picked him up. I thought we could spend the night together." Angel made her presence known.

"Cari, were you ready to come home?" I asked, ignoring her.

"Not really, but I know you were starting to miss me," he joked. I could tell it was the other way around by the way he was holding onto my leg, hugging it tightly.

"I missed you, too." Angel smiled, walking up to me.

"Let me help him put his things away," I said, ushering Cari upstairs to his room. Placing his book bag down, I asked him to join me back downstairs because I wanted to talk to him about something before knocking on the bedroom door of the room Bradleigh occupied. I wanted to get her attention before walking in the room. "Brad!" I called out.

"Yes?" she questioned, emerging from underneath the covers. I smiled as her wild dreads covered her face. She spoke in the opposite direction than where I was standing.

"I'm over this way," I chuckled.

"Oh," she giggled while moving her hair out of the way before turning to face me.

"Do you mind coming downstairs with me?"

"Um, yeah, give me a minute. Let me get myself together." She faintly smiled, running her hands through her dreads.

"Cool," I said, exiting the room.

Going back downstairs, I found Angel in the kitchen, popping popcorn. Ba'Cari looked through the entertainment center for a movie to watch.

"Daddy, what do you want to watch? *The Pursuit of Happiness*, *Harry Potter* or *Akeelah and the Bee*?"

"Um, Za'Cari, who is this?" Angel entered the living room with the popcorn in one hand, pointing at Bradleigh with the other. She didn't try to hide the fact that she had an attitude.

"Come here, Brad," I spoke, reaching my hand out for her to come to me.

"Someone needs to explain to me what the fuck is going on." Angel slammed the bowl of popcorn on my glass table, almost causing me to lose my shit. "Why is this little young bitch standing in the middle of your living room, dressed all comfortable and shit in your clothes? Is this what you been doing all weekend, playing house with some child?"

"Angel, you better bring it down several fucking notches! The only person I need to be explaining what the fuck is going on in my house to is my son. As a matter of fact, Angel, you can leave. We're about to have a family meeting."

"Oh, so I'm not family now?" Angel questioned. I could tell she was hurt.

"Man, you're doing too much, but since you wanna go there, no, you're not family; you're on my payroll. Angel, you're nothing more than Ba'Cari's nanny." I fucked with Angel tough, but she needed to be put back in her place. I wasn't feeling her attitude and how she was disrespecting someone who I had as a guest in my home. I could tell Brad wanted to speak up by her body language, but she remained quiet.

"Nothing more than the nanny, but you share your bed with me a least a few nights out of the week?" Angel sassed.

She had to really be intimidated by Bradleigh's presence because she never flipped out like this over females. "Angel, man, you know the deal, so please don't play yourself. You know what, you're right, you need to hear my announcement as well." Walking over to Ba'Cari with Brad's hand still in mine, I sat next to my son. "Ba'Cari, this is my friend, Bradleigh. She's kind of going through something and needs our help, so she'll be staying with us for a while in the guest room. Is that okay with you?" The whole time I spoke, Ba'Cari never took his eyes off Bradleigh.

"Yes, I'm fine with it!" he smiled. "It's a pleasure to meet you." Ba'Cari extended his hand out to her to shake. "What did he say your name was? Beautiful, is it?"

"You're such a little charmer." Bradleigh lightly giggled, shaking his hand. "My name is Bradleigh, and it's a pleasure to meet you as well."

"Welcome. Our home is now your home." Ba'Cari took his charm one step further by kissing her hand, causing Brad and I to laugh.

"It's not okay with me," Angel added.

"I don't believe I asked for your opinion on the matter. The only reason you're still here is because I want you to know Brad will be staying here, and you will show her the same respect you show me."

"I don't have to show her anything."

"If you want to continue being an employee of mine, you most definitely will. Showing her respect is the only option you have."

"Oh, really? So, since when have you started allowing your pick of the weeks to move right on in?"

"Cari, go upstairs and take your shower for bed," I said, dismissing my son.

"I thought we were going to watch movies?" he asked disappointedly.

"We are, after your shower."

"Okay!" I watched my son leave the living room. The moment I knew he was out of earshot, I laid into Angel's ass.

"First off, Angel, you know damn well I don't play that loud talking, neck rolling, ghetto ass shit around my son. Secondly, don't keep fucking questioning me like you pay any of the fucking bills around this motherfucker. I pay all the motherfucking bills in this house that I'm allowing Bradleigh to stay in until she's good and ready to leave. You're nothing more than Ba'Cari's nanny, who I enjoy fucking. Don't think too much of the bullshit. I'm not fucking Bradleigh, I'm helping her. Not that I need to explain my-fucking-self to you, seeing that I'm paying you to take care of my son, not be all up in my fucking business. Don't fuck up your money by being jealous over a nigga who doesn't belong to you."

"Whatever, Za'Cari, I'm leaving." Angel stormed out of the living room, wiping away her tears. Did I want to see Angel cry? No! I fucked with her, she did a good job with my son, but it was clear I needed to set some boundaries because Angel's ass was too comfortable, and I didn't like how she was talking to me like I was her man and not her boss.

"Angel!" I called out, chasing after her. She was moving so fast, she was halfway out the door.

"What, Zay?"

"What the fuck are you crying for?"

"You must really like her. You've never disrespected me over any female."

"Naw, shorty, I'm just showing you the same amount of respect you just showed my guest and me. You started tripping before I could even explain the situation. It's not what you're thinking. I'm not about to put her business out there, just know she needs help, and I will be the one doing so."

"I just need to know there's still you and I," Angel cried.

"You know, I'm starting to rethink what the fuck we're doing as well. I can't have you acting like I'm your nigga because we're fucking. I told you from the jump I didn't want to cross that line because you're Ba'Cari's nanny, but you said you could handle it. These tears let me know you're not handling the shit too well."

"No, no, Zay, don't! I just had a moment. I know you mess with other women besides me, I'm just not feeling the idea of them making themselves at home," she pouted.

"There's nothing sexual going on between Bradleigh and me. As long as everyone plays their role, everything will be straight."

"Okay," she said, rolling her eyes.

"I'm glad we're on the same page. Goodnight."

"Wait, we're not going to have movie night?"

"We are, but you're not, keep it moving. I'm not feeling all that loud talking you were doing. We'll try to have a better day tomorrow." I turned to walk back inside my house. Angel stood there, looking dumbfounded, so I motioned, letting her know to get off my porch. I could tell she was about to start crying again, but this time, I didn't care to stop her.

Angel and I had been friends for about three years now. I always used to see her around the way, hanging out, and I thought she was a cool chick. She started working for me, helping take care of Ba'Cari about two years ago when my work schedule became too much. About a year ago, we crossed the line by sleeping together. It was one of my many drunken nights. I didn't see anything in the club worth taking home—shit, maybe I had but was too drunk to notice—so I went home alone. When I got home, I was horny as fuck, and I knew Angel was feeling me, so I crossed the line by fucking her. Angel was something like in-house pussy. No matter how many bitches I fucked throughout the week, I knew she would always be there ready. Sometimes her attitude got out of hand, like it had tonight because Angel felt like she was my main bitch out of my many of bitches. I appreciated her help with Ba'Cari, and I really had to fuck with Angel to allow her to take care of my son, but as far as our relationship went, I didn't want anything exclusive with her. I just appreciated the great job she was doing taking care of my son when I couldn't, and I liked fucking her from time to time.

"So, let me know what my role is in all of this, so I can play it well," Bradleigh spoke from behind me as I locked the front door.

"What do you mean?"

"You said as long as everyone plays their role, everything will be straight, so what's mine?"

"I was more so talking to Angel. I needed her to know she was nothing more than a job. I pay her to take care of my son, I don't pay her to manage my household. I needed to remind her that her role was to be Ba'Cari's nanny, not Za'Cari's girl, but you do have a role as well. You need to be thinking about a game plan. You're more than welcome to stay here until you get on your feet. How far along are you?"

"Four months."

"You have five more months to get your shit together. No pressure, but pressure. You need more than just a duffle bag full of baby shit before your baby enters into this world. I'm willing to help you as much as I can as long as you're willing to help yourself. We'll go out tomorrow to get you some clothes and shit."

"Za'Cari, I have a plan. I've been having a plan since I was a freshman in high school. I have to make some adjustments." She smiled down at her belly, rubbing it before looking back up at me. "I still have a plan. I start school next month at the University of Louisville, I'm majoring in art." This was my first time seeing a genuine smile out of her.

"Well, that's a great start."

"Daddy, are y'all ready?" Cari came running back into the living room.

"We'll talk later," I let Brad know.

"So, what movie are we watching," I asked Ba'Cari.

"How about we let our beautiful guest choose."

Bradleigh giggled. At eight years old, my boy was already a charmer. He knew how to make a girl feel special, no matter the age. This was a quality about him I hope he kept as he got older. He was so smart and charming, and more put together than a lot of grown niggas I knew. Hell, some days, he had more sense than me. I wanted him to be a better man than me, and my son was well on the right path.

"I would love to watch *Harry Potter*." Bradleigh smiled at Ba'Cari.

"Harry Potter it is," I said, popping in the DVD.

"Can I get y'all anything out of the kitchen before the movie starts?" Bradleigh offered.

"No, you rest yourself. Whatever you need, I got you. I'll get it." Cari quickly shut Brad down.

"I got it player, player," I laughed. "You relax as well," I spoke, walking into the kitchen, opening our junk food cabinet. I pulled out chips, candy and Little Debbie cupcakes. I took those into the living room before grabbing three pops and three bottles of waters from the refrigerator. Knowing Ba'Cari, this was going to be a long movie night, so before taking the drinks into the living room, I placed a frozen pizza in the oven.

"Dad, I'll get the blankets." Ba'Cari took off running out the living room, while I moved the coffee table to the side.

Bradleigh looked puzzled as I started moving furniture around. Movie night was normal for my son and me; we loved being comfortable while enjoying movies.

"Dad, I grabbed the air mattress." Ba'Cari stumbled into the living room, struggling to carry the mattress. "Oh my, let me help you with that." Bradleigh quickly hopped to her feet to assist Ba'Cari with the mattress.

"Cari, she's too old for you, stop trying to show off," I laughed. He was doing the most.

"Age ain't nothing but a number." He winked at her.

"Age is more than a number, and it can land you behind bars," I laughed.

"Sometimes the risk is worth it." Ba'Cari winked at her again, causing her to laugh.

"Man, go get the damn blankets." I shook my head, trying not to laugh.

"I'll be back."

"You have trouble on your hands," she giggled.

"Tell me about it." I laughed before blowing up the air mattress.

"Let me help. I don't feel right watching y'all do all the work." Bradleigh helped make up the bed.

After the bed was all made up, I started the movie, while Brad and Cari got comfortable on the mattress. Cari rested at the foot of the bed, closer to the TV, while Brad and I laid at the top. I placed the bowl of popcorn and bag of Doritos between us.

Brad and Cari were all into the movie while I looked down at my phone, reading the text messages from Angel. She called herself trying to apologize, but in the same sentence, wanted to know what was going on in my household. I could tell Bradleigh staying here would be a problem for her.

Feeling the bed move, I looked over at Bradleigh. "What's good, lil' mama?"

"I see that you're occupied, so I was going to grab the pizza out of the oven."

"I got it." Going into the kitchen, I cut the pizza into four big slices. Grabbing three plates, I placed a piece on each before reentering the living room.

"Here, Car," I called out to him. He was so into the movie, he didn't hear me. Handing Bradleigh her plate, I called out to Ba'Cari again, "Ba'Cari!"

"Sir?" He looked over his shoulder for a split second.

"Your pizza."

"Thank you." He climbed back up to the head of the bed to sit next to Bradleigh.

I listened to them talk about the movie while we ate our pizza. I really didn't care too much about Harry Potter, but I watched the shit because it was something my son loved. There were so many different films, it was hard for me to keep up with all the shit going on. I could tell Ba'Cari was excited to talk to someone who knew what he was talking about. After eating, I cleaned up our mess. I was ready to get comfortable, and there was junk food everywhere. I guess Ba'Cari and Bradleigh were on the same thing I was on. When I returned from the kitchen, they were both comfortably under the cover. Cari was back at the foot end of the mattress. The moment I laid down, my eyes grew heavy, and before I knew it, a nigga was drifting off to sleep.

Waking up a few hours later, I felt someone curled under me. Since being locked up, Cari had been stuck to a nigga's hip like glue. Looking down, I was surprised to see it was Bradleigh curled up under me. I couldn't see her face because it was buried in my chest and her arm was wrapped around my waist. I was conflicted on if I should wake her up or not. Looking down at her, I realized she was now looking up at me.

"I'm sorry." She looked embarrassed, raising up.

"You're good, lil' mama."

"Goodnight."

"You don't have to leave."

"Goodnight." She avoided eye contact, racing off to her room.

I wasn't surprised by the way she had rushed off. I was surprised she even decided to join us for movie night. I think it was Cari's charm that had her letting her guard down. I wasn't going to pressure her to open up; I was going to move on her time. I didn't want to make her uncomfortable. I knew having Bradleigh around would get interesting.

7

RORY

When I first came home from overseas, I envisioned coming home to peace. The moment I stepped off the plane, it seemed like I was thrown right into Zoo and Ramsey's relationship beef. Moments after that, I met Boss, and everything between us happened fast. Ramsey finding out she was pregnant, Luna being kidnapped, Jen and all her mess, plus, on top of that, finding out I was pregnant as well; I just needed a break from everything and everyone. I called to check on Ramsey, yet I didn't step foot out the comfort of my home. Annoyingly, Boss wouldn't stop blowing me up. I didn't want anything to do with him, so I chose not to answer. I wanted him to know he had served his purpose in my life without me saying it.

I loved everything about my new home. Being in the military had my life going nonstop, so I never had the privilege to get comfortable and settle down. After weeks of being cooped up in my home, I was finally getting the peace I had longed for. All I did was sleep, and today was no different; I was in and out. The only time I got out of bed was to use the bathroom and eat.

I called myself catching up on all my favorite TV shows, plus some new ones, but I was finding it hard to keep my eyes open. I had fallen asleep watching reruns of *Moesha*. I was having a great dream, but whoever was calling my phone wouldn't let me be great.

"What the fuck?" I yelled out because whoever it was on the other end insisted on blowing my phone up. I tried to ignore it the first two times it rang, but I guess whoever was calling really needed to get in touch with me.

"Hello?" My tone was everything but nice. I didn't feel the need to open my eyes because I planned to rush whoever was on the other end off the phone so I could get back to sleep.

"Hello, may I speak to Rory?"

"This is she."

"Rory, this is Kiana. You might not know who I am, but—"

"Aw, nah, bitch," I said, cutting her off. "Let me stop you there. My nanna used to play Shirley Brown's "Woman to Woman" on repeat, so I know where you thought you were going with this, but let me stop you by saying, not today, bitch."

"Listen, I was going through my man's phone and saw your number pop up several times on his call log, so, woman to woman, I think it's only fair that I call you and let you know where I'm coming from."

"So, you're just going to finish off this outdated-ass speech when I clearly told you not today, bitch?"

"It's only fair I let you know Boss is mine."

"Listen, honey, it's not me that you need to convince. Your remake of the woman to woman speech is cute and all, but before you called, I was sleeping, and I would like to get back to it. I don't want your nigga, and when he calls my phone again, I'll make sure to give you a call. He was only supposed to be a one-night stand; now he won't go away. Now I also have to deal with his bitch playing on my damn phone. You know how you open your door for a split second and a damn fly gets in, and now you have this annoying-ass fly, flying around your house, working every bit of your nerves? Well, that's Boss." I laughed. "Now, if you would be so kind, this baby is kicking my ass, sucking all the energy out of me. So, if you don't get off my line with the bullshit so I can get some rest, I will be showing up at your doorstep, and it wouldn't be on any woman to woman talking, I'll be kicking your ass for fucking up my sleep. Next time you feel the need to have a heart to heart talk with someone, talk to your nigga. Don't call my damn phone anymore," I said before hanging up. The nerve of this bitch, waking me from my sleep for some bullshit. I wasn't about to let Boss and his bitch stress me, which was why it was no problem with me drifting back off to sleep.

When I heard banging on my front door thirty minutes later, it was no secret who was raising hell on the other side. I didn't move a muscle. Just like I didn't care too much about entertaining his bitch, I didn't feel like entertaining him. I laid there until I heard the banging stop. Closing my eyes, I tried to go back to sleep.

"Wake your ass up," Boss yelled, scaring the shit out of me. I covered my stomach as this fool dove on top of me.

"What the fuck, Boston!" I yelled, pushing him over to the side before he could land on top of me. "You need to be careful, and how the hell did you know where I live, and how the hell did you get in my house?"

"Why do I need to be careful? Is there something you would like to tell me?"

"No, you know I don't hold my tongue for anyone, so if there was something I needed to tell you, you would know."

"When were you going to tell me you were pregnant? Or was it a secret?" he asked, roughly pulling the cover back, raising my shirt. I was only nine weeks pregnant, but you could tell my belly was forming.

"It's not a secret. Everyone who needs to know, knows. I wasn't going to tell you because it's not your concern."

"Is there a possibility it's my baby?"

"Listen, there's not a possibility it's your baby, it's a known fact, but here's the thing; this is not about to be what you think."

"What does that mean?" he asked, raising his voice.

"This baby I'm carrying is mine and mine alone. I'm not interested in you being a part of my life or my baby's life."

"Bitch, are you crazy?" Boss jumped from my bed. His quick and sudden movements had me reaching in my nightstand for my gun.

"First off, I'ma need you to lower your voice before this shit goes left for you. Nigga, I will off your ass, and I won't do a day. You were a one-night stand; please don't overstay your welcome," I said, picking up my phone. Calling back the last number that had popped up on my call history, I waited for an answer.

"Hello?"

"Bitch, I'ma kick your ass when I find you. Didn't I tell you I was trying to get some rest, and here come your so-called nigga, banging on my damn door. If you don't want to be attending his funeral, you better call your dog home," I yelled into the phone before hanging up.

Moments later, Boss' phone rang. "Hello?" he answered, putting the call on speakerphone.

"Where are you at?" she asked.

"Bitch, I just told you where he was. Either you're playing dumb, or you really are," I yelled.

"I'll be home once I'm done talking to Rory."

"Really, Boss? You're not even going to try to hide that you're cheating on me?"

"Cheated, bitch, as in once. Don't be adding the I-N-G like this is something ongoing. I want his crazy ass to stay away from me just as bad as you do."

"Boss, I can't do it anymore. You're never going to change. She can have you."

"No, no, no, bitch. You will not be leaving his ass today. He's sorry, and I can promise you for him it won't happen again."

Boss hung up on Kiana before she could respond.

"Why are you acting like I didn't give you the best night of your life?" He smiled, walking into my personal space.

"It was a means to my madness." I backed away.

"You're telling me you planned to be my baby mama?"

"I planned my baby. You weren't really apart of the plan, but when I saw you in the club, I thought, yeah, he would do."

"So, you trapped me?"

"How could I trap you when you never thought to put on a rubber? You knew the possibilities of what could happen. How many rounds did you go without strapping up?"

He didn't answer as his lips crashed into mine. I enjoyed the kiss for a little while before pulling away. "Stop."

"Naw, you stop fucking playing with me." Laying me back down on the bed, Boss fought to remove my clothes as I fought him back, wanting him to stop. "Do I need to show you who's boss?" he asked, roughly grabbing my face. His lips found mine again. His hands found their way into my panties, breaking down my will to fight.

"I want you to know, this plan you think you have for your life is dead. Stop trying to play me for some joker-ass nigga. Did you really think I would be okay with knowing I had a kid out here and not being a part of their life? And if you ever pull a gun out on me again, I will fuck you up," Boss spoke as he nibbled on my ear. I moaned once he entered me.

I didn't plan on fucking him, but Boss had a way of making me do what he said when his hands and lips were on my body. That was why I tried my hardest to avoid his ass. I wouldn't answer his calls, and I avoided seeing him in person, and this was my reason why.

"I have to be gentle with your body now since you're carrying my baby." He had a medium speed going. I felt like I was under his spell. He stared into my eyes so intensively before passionately kissing me. "We got to stop this," I cried out.

"Ro, we're just getting started. We in this shit for life," he said, picking up his pace. I was really trying to convince myself. His dick was too good to let go, but this wasn't a part of the plan. Boss made me cum several times before leaving me because Kiana wouldn't stop blowing up his phone. I didn't regret my baby, but I had a feeling shit in my life was about to be hectic. Boss was going to be a problem.

8

BRADLEIGH

I was stressed because this wasn't the first time I'd met the man who had rescued me from sleeping in the park about a month ago. Like I had explained before, I was tired of living a sheltered life, so I began to do things I had no business doing. Being in a twenty-one and older club was one.

On this particular day, four months ago, my older sister, Shani, came over and I lifted her ID from her wallet. We were practically identical, so I knew I could pull off using her ID.

My parents were all about my studies, so when I told them I was staying the night at a classmate's house to study, they were all for it. I knew my parents would be disappointed if they knew what I was really up to, but I couldn't think about that; all I wanted to do was live for me.

I told my parents I wanted to get a head start on my studies, so they weren't suspicious when I left my home in the middle of the evening. With my book bag in tow, I hopped in my car, waving lovingly at my parents as they stood in the doorway, waving back. My parents thought I was such an angel, and that was why it was so easy to pull the wool over their eyes sometimes. I didn't make it a habit of defying my parents; most of the time, I did what was asked of me, but with my eighteenth birthday quickly approaching, I began to develop this "I'm grown can't nobody tell me anything" attitude.

Feeling like I had gotten away with murder, I made my way to my P.O. box that my parents knew nothing about to pick up my packages. I had ordered some sexy clothes online. My style normally consisted of church clothes, or when I lounged around the house, I wore clothes two sizes too big. Thanks to not being able to do too much, I spent a lot of my time browsing the net. I had my own credit card, but seeing that the bank statement came in the mail addressed to my father, I couldn't just buy what I wanted without getting caught up. It was crazy what I had to go through just to live a little. In order to order my clothes online without getting caught, I had to purchase a prepaid card to use. Withdrawing two hundred dollars off my credit card, I told my father I used the money to purchase new church attire. I didn't feel guilty about lying because I was partially telling the truth. I did spend the money on clothes, just not clothes he would approve of.

During one of my times of sneaking out of the house, I had met a girl named Bonnie. She was twenty-two, and after hanging out a few times, she invited me out to the club. She believed I was twenty-one because that was the age I had told her. After leaving my P.O. box, I made my way to her house. She lived in the heart of the hood, and that excited me. Her life was so much different from mine; something was always going on around her way. Although sometimes fights broke out, everyone in her neighborhood considered each other family, unlike in my neighborhood. Sometimes you could barely get a hello out of my uptight, bougie-ass neighbors.

We sat on Bonnie's porch most of the day to pass the time. I got entertainment being in the hood; so much stuff happened in the first hour of us chilling on Bonnie's porch. Some dude had gotten caught by his girlfriend with his side chick. I hate to say it, but I got a sick joy out of watching the drama. Never once did the girlfriend blame her man for being out in the streets, doing her wrong. Her main focus was beating the hell out of his side chick. That drama only bought the neighborhood out; I wasn't the only one who loved some good drama.

I texted my mother a few times just to check in and not raise any suspicion. Around nine o'clock, I texted my mom I loved her, and I was going to bed before getting ready for the club.

Bonnie said she had a going out ritual that she lived by before going out to the club, and I had to live by it as well. She blasted loud music to get her mood right, and she did a lot of smoking and drinking. I had accepted the drink, but I wasn't a smoker. My pop-pop had died from lung cancer because he was a heavy smoker, so that really wasn't my thing.

I wanted to truly look the part of a twenty-one-year-old, so I had to take some extra steps for this to go over smoothly. I didn't wear makeup much because my father didn't think it was suitable for a "child", but what he didn't know was I often bought makeup from Sephora behind his back. Although I didn't get to wear it out in public, I often applied it in the privacy of my bedroom. I wouldn't call myself a makeup artist or anything, but then again, art was my specialty, so beating my face came naturally. I had to buy a wig because Shani had shoulder length, sandy brown hair.

Braiding my dreads up in twelve different braided plaits, I wrapped the braid around in a beehive style with bobby pins before placing a cap over them. Bonnie allowed me to get ready in her spare bedroom, so I had my own space to get dressed. After laying the outfit I wanted to wear tonight on the bed, I took a shower. After, I perfectly applied my makeup and installed my wig unit; it was a straight, sandy brown wig with a middle part. My hair and makeup had me feeling something I had never felt before: sexy. Once I slid into my dress, I started feeling myself on a whole 'nother level. I thought the dress was hot once I saw it online, but seeing it on my body was everything. I hid behind big clothes so much, I had forgotten I had a nice set of titties and an amazing ass. Tonight, my assets wouldn't go unnoticed, thanks to this revealing dress. I was wearing a red, fitted halter top. I loved it so much because the front and back were cut out. I was feeling the way my breasts looked.

After getting dressed and telling each other how sexy we both looked, we were out the door, and off to the club. I decided to drive my own car because I had plans to sneak into my house after I had left the club, and that was why I didn't plan to overdo it with the alcohol.

I tried not to act so excitedly after we were finally granted entry into the club. My parents didn't really let me hang out—church functions were the closest I got to a party—so being in the club did something to my body. I didn't want to come off immature to Bonnie, so I kept my cool. I knew the excitement danced around in my eyes as I looked around at all the partygoers. I watched as half-naked women sashayed past me, carrying a tray with a bucket full of bottles and sparkles.

I had no clue we were attending a birthday party until I heard the DJ come over the microphone, giving the birthday boy a shout out.

"Bitch, this shit is jumping!" Bonnie yelled in my ear over the music. I still had to get used to Bonnie using the word bitch as a term of endearment.

"I know!" I said, looking around. People were either holding up the wall or freak dancing on the floor.

"Let's dance!" Bonnie pulled my arm, leading me to the dance floor.

Tensing up, I became hesitant. I was so excited about coming to the club, it had just hit me that I was missing a key ingredient: I didn't know how to dance. Bonnie swayed her hips from side to side to the music as she held my hand, easing our way through the crowd.

Looking around, I tried to move my body the best I could to the beat. I didn't come to stand around, so I decided to give dancing a try. I guess I wasn't doing a bad job as I listened to Bonnie hype me up, causing me to dance harder.

I was having so much fun dancing with Bonnie, I was caught off guard by someone roughly slapping my butt like they had the right.

"God damn, devil in the red dress," the person who had smacked my butt said before drinking straight from the champagne bottle he held in his hand.

"Excuse me?" I asked with an attitude with my hands on my hips.

"That ass is looking right, I couldn't help myself. Your ass was looking right, but damn, I'm feeling you even more from the front." He took his thumb, running it down my cheek, letting it linger. He made his way down to my breasts, causing me to back away.

"I repeat, excuse you? What do you think you're doing? You can't just walk around, touching women without their permission!" I yelled.

"His bad, shorty. He's drunk. Shit, we're drunk! It's my motherfucking birthday!" another dude yelled. I was so caught up in his little friend thinking he could get free feels in, I didn't see him standing there.

"Being drunk is no excuse."

"Relax, shorty, bitches get their ass felt on every day, B," the friend spoke, causing them both to laugh. Both tossed their bottles back at the same time, downing the champagne. It was clear they were both passed drunk and didn't need another drop of liquor.

"Y'all can't be serious?" I questioned. These two were being disrespectful, and that was something I wasn't used to.

"Ease up, my little devil." The guy who had touched my ass tried to reach out and touch my face again.

"Stop calling me that." I smacked his hand away.

"You're too uptight. Go to the bar and tell them Zay sent you. Anything you and your girl want is on me. After you loosen up, come find me."

"She will," Bonnie said, quickly pulling me away at the mention of free drinks. She didn't pull me away fast enough because he ended up smacking my butt again. I shot him a look before he disappeared into the crowd.

"Oh my gosh, Brad, that's Zay, and the other dude was his brother, Zoo!" Bonnie was excited, and I didn't get why.

"Okay, who is he? Who are they?" I asked, not impressed.

"You're about to find out. It seems like Zay is feeling the devil in the red dress," she teased.

"Not interested." I rolled my eyes. I had no clue who this guy was; I barely even paid attention to what he looked like.

"We'll see! Now, what are we drinking?" Bonnie gave me a smirk. I didn't like the knowing look she was giving me.

"What can I get for you ladies?" the bartender yelled out.

I didn't drink, so I had no clue what to order, so I allowed Bonnie to do the ordering for us. "Let us get a bottle of Grey Goose with two cups of ice, compliments of Zay," Bonnie smiled.

"Coming right up." The bartender smiled back.

I didn't want to accept the drink offer because I didn't want this guy to think I owed him anything. Bonnie was drinking before I could speak up. Finding a table, Bonnie and I enjoyed the bottle, the music, and each other's company. Bonnie was doing a lot of drinking, yet she was holding herself together well. I was more so nursing my drink, seeing that I still needed to drive home, and I didn't know my limits on how much I could drink.

After a while, I drugged Bonnie back on the dance floor. I was tired of sitting around. Bonnie was a good time, and I loved her energy. I watched the way she moved her body, so I mocked her movement. I was having so much fun. If my dad knew what I was doing, he would have a heart attack.

I didn't know much about hip-hop music, so I didn't understand why all the females in the club flipped when the beat dropped, and a dude said, "I got a lot of cash, and I don't mind spending it," before he began to rap. I didn't know this song, but the artist was talking about sex, and the beat sounded like a bed was squeaking.

I danced along anyway. I didn't want people to know I didn't listen to urban music. I was playing a part tonight.

"Do you like the way I flick my tongue or nah?" I heard someone whisper in my ear as their tongue grazed my ear. Looking over my shoulder, I realized it was the Zay guy.

"You can ride my face until you're drippin' cum (drippin' cum)
Can you lick the tip then throat the dick or nah? (can you do it, baby)
Can you let me stretch that pussy out or nah?

I'm not the type to call you back tomorrow," Zay sang along with the song in my ear. I was feeling all kinds of emotions as his hands moved all over my body.

"I thought I told you to come find me?" he asked, turning me to face him. His hands went right to my behind.

"You did, but I don't answer to you."

"You don't? You didn't have a problem listening to what a nigga had to say when I told you to hit the bar, drinks on me."

I didn't say anything as I took in this man's features. I didn't have a type, but if I did, this man invading my personal space would be perfect. There was a loud voice in my head screaming for me to run away, but my feet wouldn't move. I was a church girl, so it wasn't hard for me to spot a bad boy. My father had groomed me to spot the sign of a bad boy and to steer clear of them, yet here I was, standing in the middle of the club, wrapped up in a bad boy's arms.

It was no secret that Zay's mood was nice, thanks to the excessive amount of liquor he had drunk. I could tell he was drunk the moment I turned around when he first approached me. Him being drunk was the reason I didn't take his request to come find him serious. He probably walked through the club telling several women that before approaching me.

His body was towering over mine, so I had to look up to get a good look at his face. He had his cap pulled down low, but I could still see his slightly bushy eyebrows and low eyes. A hoop, gold nose ring rested on the right side of his nose. He also had one in his ear. A neatly trimmed mustache rested over the top of his perfectly-shaped lips. The way he smirked at me, showing off his white teeth behind his sexy smile had my heart racing. His lips looked so soft and tempting. My father would lose it if he knew I was interacting with someone who looked like Zay. His freshly cut, chinstrap beard and the tattoos that covered his neck all the way down to his hands had me ready to lose this purity ring I had tucked away in my backpack. Everything about him screamed hood nigga down to his attire, and I liked it.

When he leaned down to kiss my neck, I was slightly shocked. "I'm ready to go, and I'm in no condition to drive. You got me?" he asked, whispering and nibbling on my ear at the same time.

I wanted to speak, but nothing would come out. The feelings that ran through my body were all over the place. I was in complete lust for this man right now. I guess he didn't need me to speak. Grabbing my hand, Zay told Bonnie I was leaving before we made our way toward the exit. I guess he didn't care to tell his peoples he was leaving.

"Lead the way to your car," Zay said, checking me out in the night light. I could tell he was trying to see if I was beautiful past his beer goggles.

I tried to let go of his hand, but he wasn't having that. I was breaking so many rules tonight. Not only was I at a place I had no business being, but I was also riding in my car with a MAN, knowing that my father had a "no boys allowed in my car" rule.

"Where do you live?" I asked, looking over at Zay the moment I stopped at the first red light.

After rattling off his address, I started to type it into my GPS. Knowing that my father sometimes checked it, I thought otherwise. I would just have to ask him for directions on the way.

"Am I going the right way?" I asked Zay, taking my eyes off the road briefly. To my surprise, he was sleep. "Zay!" I called out his name several

times, not getting any answers, causing me to panic. "Zay, wake up!" I shook him, getting nothing but light snores in return.

"Really? Just my luck," I whined. I didn't know what I was thinking leaving the club with a man I didn't even know.

Making a U-turn, I made my way downtown. I wanted to take him back to the club and let his brother deal with him, but looking at the time on the dashboard, I realized the party was now over. I wanted to reach into his pocket for his wallet to get his license out, but I didn't want to invade his privacy. The only thing I could think of was checking into a hotel. I refused to drive around until I found my destination.

The first hotel I spotted was the Hampton, so I stopped. I tried waking Zay up again with no such luck before going in to pay for the room. My plan was to go back to Bonnie's to change my clothes before sneaking into my house. I was going to change here and leave Zay here to sleep his night off. He could call a cab or a ride to take him home in the morning.

"Hey!" I shook Zay. "Hey, wake up." I shook him a little harder.

"Zay, wake up and get out of the car."

"What's up, man?"

"We're here."

"Where exactly is here, because this is not the address I gave you."

"Clearly, it's a hotel," I said, allowing my frustration to show. I was tired. I'd had a great night, but I was ready to get it over with, and babysitting a grown man I didn't know was not how I thought it would end. "I tried to wake you to get directions to your home, but you sleep like you're in a coma so this will be your home for the night. Let's go, so I can get going," I said before grabbing my overnight bag from the backseat.

Zay stumbled a few feet behind me after we got off the elevator, making our way to the room. I shook my head, confused on how my night had gotten here. Zay stood closely behind as I looked through my purse for the hotel key. "What are you shaking your head about?" he asked, resting his soft lips on my neck. That caused me to understand how my night had gotten here. I got caught prisoner by the way his touch felt. I could feel him hiking my dress up slowly, and I did nothing to stop him. I was not myself tonight; could I blame it on the alcohol?

"Find the key," he demanded as his hands caressed my inner thighs.

I felt dizzy as I looked around my purse for the key. This man had my mind all out of focus because the hotel key sat right in my face. With his hand traveling between my legs, and his lips on my neck, it was hard for me to think clearly.

The moment the door opened, Zay wasted no time guiding me to the bed. By now, my dress was halfway up. Removing his hat, I found another reason to feel like he was the sexiest man I'd ever laid eyes on. His hair was so perfect. Running my hands through his hair, it was so soft and wavy.

Zay buried his head in the crook of my neck, and I got nervous when I felt his tongue brush up against my neck. All these feelings were new to me. My nervousness increased when I felt his hands rub up against my private. I could feel the fabric of my thong getting wet.

I knew what was taking place was wrong on so many levels, but I didn't have it in me to tell Zay to stop. Ending my night at a hotel wasn't a part of my grand plan.

I moaned once I felt his hand slide into my panties. I'd never done drugs before, but I'm pretty sure this is what a high felt like. My eyes felt so lazy the harder Zay sucked on my neck, and the more he moved his digits around inside me made it difficult to keep my eyes open.

"Take this shit off," he demanded, tugging at my dress before removing his own clothes.

I was hesitant. I loved the way he made my body feel, but I didn't think I was ready for this.

"What's wrong?" he asked before his lips crashed into mine. I could taste the alcohol on his tongue.

"Nothing." I released a moan.

"So, what's the holdup? Get naked." Zay took it upon himself to unhook my dress. Pulling my dress down, he exposed my bare breasts.

"Pretty-ass titties." He smiled, melting my heart. Taking both of my breasts in each of his hands, he took his time showing each one attention with his tongue. I ran my hands over his waves.

Pulling me back on the bed, Zay positioned his body over mine. I wanted to feel his lips against mine again, so I leaned up to kiss him, and while doing so, he removed my thong.

Was I ready for this?

I didn't have time to decide if I was ready or not because Zay did that for me. His penis head was at my opening before I could finish my thoughts. I braced myself for the pain. Zay kissed my lips while pushing inside of me. "Ohh," I moaned into his mouth. He continued to passionately kiss me as he worked his way inside of my tight tunnel. I tried to keep my whining to a minimum. I didn't want to give myself away; I had to take it like a big girl.

"Fuck!" Zay slightly raised his body off mine. Placing his hands firmly on the bed, he quickened his pace. I didn't recognize the sound of my own voice as nonstop moans slipped from my mouth. Was it possible to feel pleasure and pain at the same time?

Zay continued to rock in and out of me until his body collapsed on mine. All you could hear was both of our heavy breathing throughout the room. Taking a breather was short-lived; we went at it for a few more hours before Zay fell back into a drunken slumber. Me, on the other hand, I stayed up thinking about everything that had taken place tonight, and my guilt was starting to set in. Rushing to the bathroom, I quickly showered before getting dressed. Looking at my purity ring, I shamefully slid it back on my finger before grabbing everything that belonged to me. I took one last look at Zay before leaving out of the hotel room. Wanting to rebel and live a little had me going against everything I believed in, and I was now regretting everything I'd done. I wanted to forget this night had happened.

All was well with pretending the night with Zay had never happened until I was hit with the reality of being pregnant. I had some explaining to do, and I didn't know how Zay would take the truth.

I jumped, startled by the knocks on the bedroom door I now called my own. "Yo, Brad, you decent?" Zay called from the other side of the door.

"Um...," I stalled, not sure if I wanted to be bothered. My trip down memory lane had me afraid of coming face to face with Zay. My lies and secrets had me stressed out.

"Brad!" Zay called out again.

"Come in," I called out.

"How are you feeling today?" he asked, walking in, taking a bite out of an apple.

"Good," I spoke hesitantly.

Zay laid comfortably on my bed, taking another bite of his apple. "We need to talk."

"About?" I asked nervously. Every day, I was afraid Zay would put two and two together and remember the night we met.

"You been staying here for a while now, and I think it's time we have a talk. I've been trying to give you your space to let you come around, but you're taking forever. It's been damn near two months, and I know nothing about how you ended up almost sleeping in the park. I trust you enough to live under my roof, and I feel like you should trust me enough with your story. Who is Bradleigh? What was your life like?"

I avoided eye contact, not sure what to say. I knew this moment was coming. I had been living with Zay and Cari, yet they knew nothing about my life before I entered their home. I felt like we had built trust between one another because I tried to show them who I was as a person. I felt like that would be enough, but clearly, it wasn't; Zay wanted more. I could no longer get by on just being me; he wanted answers.

"BRAD, YOU CAN TRUST ME," he said, touching my leg, causing me to smile weakly.

"What would you like to know?" I asked, hoping he didn't ask any questions about my "child's father." But, I tried to mentally prepare myself for a story because I knew it would come up.

"I feel like I know you, but not really. I know you have a kind heart; I can tell that much by the little things you do around here," he said, biting his apple again. "I want to know more about you, like, what's your full name, birthday; shit, you can even throw your social in there. I barely know you. I need some leverage to assure me I can trust I won't wake up one day to realize you finessed me," he joked.

"Bradleigh Briana Lambert is my full name, and I'll be eighteen on October third."

"And your social security number?" he grinned before taking another bite of his apple.

Smiling back, I continued. "I grew up in the church, that's my father," I said, pointing at the television. Sadness washed over me. This was my normal routine, watching my father's sermon on TV. As much as I cried about wanting out of the church, I realized it was where I belonged. I missed it. It wasn't that I couldn't go, I was just ashamed.

Turning around to look at what I was pointing at, I watched Zay's reaction.

"That's my mother," I spoke as the camera panned around the congregation before landing on my mother.

"Tell me about your family."

"As you can see, my family is big in the church; my father is the minister at Greater Christian Baptist. My mother stands by his side as the loving, devoted, God fearing woman. My parents have been happily married for almost twenty-two years. I have a twenty-one-year-old sister, who is the closest thing that I have to a best friend named Shani." I smiled, thinking about my sister. I missed her like crazy, and every day, I wanted to pick up the phone and call her, but I didn't. I was kind of mad she hadn't fought harder, but then again, I understood; there was no point in us both being homeless. Although she lived on her own, she depended on my parents just as much as I did.

"I heard you throwing around words like loving, happily, and best friend; if that's the case, how did you end up almost sleeping in a park?"

"This is how I ended up homeless," I said, pointing at my baby bump.

"Almost homeless," he smiled, rubbing my belly. I smiled back at him, feeling a tug at my heart. Not wanting to cross that line, I got my little feelings together.

"I'm seventeen, the daughter of a rising minister, and I'm pregnant out of wedlock. I hid it as long as I could, but the night you found me in the park was the day my luck ran out. I could see the hurt and embarrassment written all over my parents' faces. My parents wanted nothing to do with me, which was expected. Nothing came before the church, not even their children. They got rid of me before the news could spread. A pregnancy scandal could ruin my father before he could really get started. I know my sister would've allowed me to stay with her, but my parents forbid it by threatening her livelihood. My sister was the only person I told about my pregnancy, and she took me to my first doctors' appointment."

"That's fucked up. Your parents are fucked up." I could tell he was upset. "What about your child's father?"

"What about him?" I asked nervously.

"Where is he? How does he feel about this?"

"I don't know," I shrugged, keeping it short. I had no clue how I would explain this situation to Zay.

"How many months are you?"

"I should be about five months. The last time I went to the doctor, I was about three months, and that was in June."

I watched Zay reach into his pocket for his phone. We listened to it ring, waiting for the person on the other end to answer.

"Hey, bro," a woman spoke cheerfully on the other end.

"What's up, Rah-Rah? I need you to do me a favor. You know I been having my peoples stay with me. Well, she's about five months pregnant. I need to find a good doctor's office to take her to. You think you can set that up for me?"

"Bitch, my girl isn't your secretary," I heard a guy yell in the background, causing the girl to giggle.

"Nigga, I didn't say she was. Stop meddling, bitch nigga." I was taken aback by their constant use of profanity. I wasn't sure if they were joking or serious.

"I got you, Zay," the girl said, interrupting their bickering.

"How the fuck you got him, and you haven't even made an appointment for yourself?"

"I'm going to do it at the same time, Zouk. Get out of my conversation! Zay, I'll call you with the place and time. I need her name and birthday."

"Okay, I'll text it to you," Zay said before hanging up. "Here, shoot her your information," Zay said, handing me his phone.

After texting my information, I handed Zay his phone back. "I'm about to head out to the barbershop; I got a few appointments. Do you need anything before I go?"

"No, I'm fine."

"Okay, if you need to go anywhere, I'll leave the keys to my other car on the kitchen counter."

"Okay, thank you." I smiled slightly.

"No problem. Call me if you need me, little one." He winked before walking out.

I tried to stop myself from blushing. I didn't want to fall for Zay because I was vulnerable at this moment. I shook my head, trying to get rid of the flashbacks I had of our night we had spent together.

"Help me, Father." I laid back on my bed, taking a deep breath.

9

RAMSEY

Things in my household finally felt right again. My babies were back home with me where they belonged. Zoo and I had talked to Luna about the kidnapping, and sadly, she had to testify against them because Lance and Jen were still clinging to being innocent. Seeing how they were going to let Nicki take the fall for everything by herself, she started to tell it all from the beginning.

Sadly, I was just now getting around to checking on the baby. After a month of Zoo's nonstop bitching, I was finally sitting in the doctor's office, waiting for my name to be called. My stomach was growing with every passing day. By the size of my belly, I had to be about six or seven months pregnant, which was shocking, seeing that the pregnancy symptoms popped up so late.

Rory accompanied Zoo and me to the doctor, hoping I would find out the sex of the baby so she could have a gender reveal party for us. Zay was also bringing the pregnant girl, who was a house guest in his home to get a check-up as well. We didn't know much about that situation, but Zay had asked me to recommend a doctor to her, so I recommended mine.

They entered the doctor's office the moment my name was called. The girl standing next to Zay was beyond beautiful, but I could tell she was young. We greeted them before making our way to the back for me to get checked out.

"Hello, Ms. Scott, I'm your nurse, Simone. How are you feeling today?"

"Fine, thanks for asking. This is my boyfriend, Zouk, and my sister, Rory."

"Nice to meet everyone. From my understanding, this is your first doctor's visit since finding out you're pregnant, correct?"

"Yes, life has been a little hectic for me."

"Okay, let's check the little one out." She blessed me with a warm smile. "Are you feeling nausea?"

"Yes, more than I would like," I pouted.

"We can give you something to help with that."

"Please, I'm tired of hearing her ass cry about it," Zoo spoke up.

"Shut up, Zouk." I rolled my eyes. Nurse Simone giggled at our bickering.

"Do you feel your baby move around?" she asked.

"Yeah, she feels the baby move a lot."

"Have you been leaking fluids, or have you had any vaginal spotting or bleeding?"

"Naw, no spotting or bleeding," Zoo answered.

"Zoo, can I get a word in?" I giggled.

"Have you been spotting or bleeding?" he asked.

"No!"

"Okay, then, is that not the answer I just gave Nurse Jackie?"

"It's Nurse Simone," she chuckled, correcting him.

"Excuse him, sometimes he can be a bit much."

"It's fine," she giggled. "Have you had any contractions?"

I looked over at Zoo, waiting for him to answer. "Don't be a smart ass, Ramsey." Zoo mean mugged me, causing me to giggle.

"I have slight pain, but nothing out of the norm."

"Okay, and from my understanding, Aunt, you're here because

you are the gatekeeper for the gender, correct? You're the only one who wants to know the sex of the baby, right?" Nurse Simone asked, lifting my shirt.

"Yes!" Rory answered excitedly.

"Man!" Zoo sighed, frustrated, shaking his head.

"I feel like you're going to be a problem. You should step out of the room, Zoo," Rory announced.

"Man," Zoo said again, getting up to leave. He knew he couldn't handle staying in the room and not knowing.

"Okay, Aunt, are you ready?" The nurse smiled, turning the screen in the opposite direction of me.

Rory stood behind the nurse with the hugest smile on her face. I watched Rory's every move, hoping I would get a hint of what I was having by her expression.

"Oh, my!" Her eyes grew big again, and I felt like this was déjà vu from having Luna and Luchi.

"Oh, my goodness, its twins again, isn't it?" I asked in a panic.

"No, it's not twins," Rory said, briefly pulling her eyes away from the computer screen.

"Oh, thank God. I wouldn't be able to handle it." I breathed a sigh of relief.

"Okay, mama, you're about five months along."

"Really?" I pouted. "I'm already big as a house." I wanted to cry seeing that I had already gained a lot of weight and still had several months to go.

"Everything looks great. I'm going to set you up another appointment for next week. Aunt, I'm going to get you an envelope." She smiled, exiting the room while Zoo reentered.

"So, what are we having?" was the first question out of Zoo's mouth.

"You'll find out Saturday, like everyone else," Rory squeaked excitedly. "I'll be waiting in the waiting room," Rory said, patting Zoo on the shoulder before walking past him, out the door.

"Whose dumb ass idea was this again? Fuck is a gender reveal party anyway? Women stay making up shit. Even when pregnant, y'all still find a way to party."

"Shut up, boy," I laughed. He was real deal mad. I wasn't about to rub salt in his wound about it, so I stayed quiet.

GENDER REVEAL PARTY

I was excited about my gender reveal party. I was glad it was finally here so Zoo could stop getting on everyone's nerves. It was driving him crazy that he wasn't in control. Rory cursed him out on a daily basis because he called her phone, talking crazy every day. I wasn't expecting a Dr. Seuss themed gender reveal party, but I loved it.

Red, white, blue and yellow decorated Rory's backyard. I wanted to greet my family and friends, but the food table caught my attention.

"Mama, look at the cake!" Luna jumped around, excited.

"I know, I love it." I smiled, admiring the yellow, white, blue and red three-tier, layered Dr. Seuss cake.

The cake topper said, "It's true, it's true! A baby is due!" The top layer, which was yellow, read, "Will it be pink?" The middle layer, which was blue, said, "Or," and the bottom layer of the cake, which was red, read, "Will it be blue?"

"Aunt Ro did good," Luna said, looking around.

"Well, thank you. Everything I touch is golden." Rory appeared out of nowhere, walking up to hug Luna, then me.

"This shit is nice and all, but let's get to it." Zoo walked up. We had only been here for a good ten to fifteen minutes, and Zoo was already on his shit.

"Nigga, eat something or mingle." Rory rolled her eyes.

"I ate before I came, and you know I hate people." He looked around, mean mugging our guests.

"Zouk, relax," I laughed, hitting him on the shoulder.

"Now you know that's hard for that nigga to do." Zay walked up, laughing as well.

"What's up, Rah-Rah?" Zay pulled me in for a hug.

"Hey, bro."

"Let me properly introduce y'all to Bradleigh."

"Brad, this is my little brother, Zoo, his girlfriend and daughter, Ramsey and Luna, and this pain in the ass is the baby sis, Rory."

"Nice to meet y'all." Bradleigh timidly spoke, avoiding eye contact.

"It's nice to meet you as well," I spoke.

"Speak for yourself, Ramsey." Angel made her presence known. I didn't miss the eye roll from Bradleigh.

"The same way you enter, Angel, you can exit. Don't start with your bullshit today," Zay barked.

"Come on, let's feed these babies." I gave Bradleigh a reassuring smile before grabbing her hand. Not only was Angel giving her hell, but Zoo was also looking at her crazy as well. I knew he had something rude to say, and that was why I quickly pulled her away before he did.

"Don't leave this baby out," Rory said, rubbing her belly. She was now three months pregnant and had a cute little baby bump.

"Thanks for saving me," Bradleigh smiled. "Angel works my nerves on a daily. It's like she comes over every day just to start stuff."

"Leave, and I won't be a problem." Angel piled a hand full of chips on her plate before walking off.

"Why does she remind me of Amber? Brad, you need to stick up for yourself, or she's going to be a big problem," I said, moving around, fixing my plate.

"I don't want to be a problem. I appreciate Za'Cari opening his home up to me. I don't want to bring any problems to his home."

"Fuck that, never be afraid to cuss a bitch out. If you allow them to try you once, they will never let up."

"Rory, she's a good church girl, stop trying to ruin her." Zay walked over, standing next to Bradleigh.

"Listen, baby, God knows your heart, and He understands sometimes you need to cuss a bitch out."

"Rory, you better hope Nanna don't hear you talking like that." I looked around, nervous, hoping my nanna wasn't close by to hear Rory's foolishness.

"Nanna would tell her the same thing. Listen to me, Bradleigh, when that bitch come at you, make sure you come back at her ass."

"Damn Rory, why I gotta be all that?" Angel asked, now standing next to Zay.

"You're acting like a bitch, so I think that's the name that best suits you," Rory said, never backing down.

Angel only rolled her eyes. She knew not to try that slick shit with Rory. Pregnant or not, Rory had no problem smacking a chick.

"See, shorty isn't as bad as she lets on." Rory winked at Bradleigh before walking off.

I only giggled back. It was clear Angel was all bark with no bite, and she only picked on Brad because she allowed her to.

"Come on, Bradleigh, let's leave them be; it's clear Angel needs a moment." I shook my head at how pressed Angel was acting. She reminded me so much of Amber, and that made me want to knock her head off her shoulders.

Walking away, I took a seat at the table with Zoo's parents and my nanna. I introduced Bradleigh to everyone. I couldn't enjoy my food because every time I looked up, Zoo was pointing at his watch, causing me to laugh. He was so impatient. Zoe went around with a video camera, getting everyone's vote on if they thought it was a boy or a girl.

"This is so cool. I wish I could've had something like this." Brad was smiling, but the joy didn't reach her eyes. She looked as if she was going to cry.

"How far along are you? Do you know what you're having?"

"I'm five months, and it's a baby girl." Her face truly lit up when she spoke.

"Well, I have my fingers crossed we'll be going baby girl shopping together."

"Hey, may I have everyone's attention!" Rory called out, breaking up our conversation. I giggled as I watched her push Boss away as he tried to stand beside her proudly like a loving boyfriend.

"Rory, you better go on, trying to play me like we didn't plan this shit together." He pulled her close to his side. "Excuse me, may I have everyone's attention. First, we would like to thank everyone for coming out," Boss announced. I cracked up because I could tell Rory was annoyed. She hated when Boss acted like they were one. It really pissed her off when he told people he was her baby daddy.

"I'm not going to keep telling you there's no we!" Rory yelled.

"Man, figure your dysfunctional-ass relationship out on your own time. Get to the fucking point of why we're here: what the sex of our baby is!" Zoo yelled. I could tell he was on the verge of snapping.

"Anyway." Rory rolled her eyes. "Who's ready to find out the sex of the baby?" Rory questioned excitedly.

I got nervous, yet excited as I watched everyone cheer. "Here you go, Ramsey and Zoo, these are for you." Rory and Boss handed Zoo and I blindfolds.

"Man, just show me the ultrasound. I'm not trying to go through all that," Zoo complained.

"Just put the damn thing on and shut up!" Rory barked, placing her hand on her hip.

"Man," he groaned, placing the blindfold on. Walking over to him, I soon followed his lead by placing the blindfold over my eyes.

My adrenaline was now pumping as I listened to our guests scream and cheer in excitement. Placing her hand inside of mine, Rory began to guide me forward.

"Remove your blindfold," she squeaked in excitement.

"Oh my goodness, I knew it." My eyes grew big as they landed on the two boxes. One read, "Thing One" and the other read, "Thing Two."

"Oh shit, nigga, this calls for a double shot of Henny." Zoo jumped around. I'd never seen him so excited.

"Before we open the boxes, I ask again, what do y'all think the sex of the babies are?" Zoe excitedly screamed. I got overwhelmed as I listened to everyone yell at once.

"Let's open the boxes and see."

My hands began to sweat as I approached the box that read, "Thing One." Luchi stood by my side while Luna stood by Zoo's side.

"Can we get a countdown from five," Luchi hyped the guests up.

"Five, four, three, two..." Luchi and I ripped the box open, revealing blue balloons as Zay shot blue confetti in the air, causing it to rain down on Luchi and I. Looking over at Zoo and Luna, their box revealed blue balloons as Crash shot his confetti gun and blue confetti rained down on them as well. Everyone cheered around us. I didn't know how I felt about having Zoo and Luchi, plus two more boys. Zoo's lips crashed into mine, roughly kissing me several times.

"Aye, aye, let me get everyone's attention. Let me get everyone to quiet down! Quiet down!" Boss yelled, getting everyone's attention again.

"Oh, did I forget to mention there is a thing three?" Rory yelled as Crash's brother, Steel, carried in the third box.

"Get the fuck out of here!" Zoo and Luchi yelled at the same time, jumping around.

"Rory, stop playing!" I groped my stomach. There is no way I was carrying three babies inside of me right now. No wonder why I looked seven months pregnant when I was only five.

"Please be a girl, please be a girl, please be a girl," Luna chanted over and over again with her fingers crossed.

"Let's get it!" Zoo yelled, clapping his hands together several times.

Luna pulled the box open, and the look of disappointment was displayed on her face as well as mine. "Thank you, Ramsey! I love you. My four boys and my princess."

"Noooooo!" I cried unhappily.

"Bro, you better fix your face. What the fuck are you crying for?" Some of Zoo's excitement washed away once he saw my reaction.

"I don't want three boys."

"Too late, now cheer the fuck up." He kissed me, washing away some of the sadness and anger.

Zay and Steel were already preparing cups of Henny and music was now blasting throughout the backyard. Everyone was celebrating. Me, on the other hand, was worried about how I was now a mother of five, and how I would survive Zoo and four reflections of him. I was already asking God for strength.

10

RORY

Surprisingly, Boss was a good baby daddy, always at my beck and call when I needed something; it was his damn girlfriend who was the problem. I hated bitches like her. She knew her nigga cheated, but instead of her addressing her man, she looked at the women he cheated with to be the problem. Her dumb ass decided to stay, which was her business. My problem was she complained while doing so. Her dumb ass stayed playing on my phone. If she wasn't crying, begging me to leave Boss alone, she would threaten to cause harm to me and my unborn.

Today, she was in rare form because I didn't send Boss home the night after the gender reveal party like I normally did. Last night, I felt like being selfish; I wanted to be held and kissed all night. For the last hour or so, Kiana had been yelling about pulling up, but she had yet to show, so I laid on the couch in her man's arms, enjoying a bowl of ice cream, watching TV.

Boss seemed to be unbothered by Kiana's threats. I didn't know too much about their relationship because I really didn't care, but what I did know was he treated her like a doormat; she took too much shit from his ass. Nigga had a whole baby on her, and she was still madly in love with his ass.

My phone rang for the hundredth time today. Reaching over me, Boss grabbed my phone off the coffee table.

"Hello?" he answered, annoyed.

"Really, Boss? You're getting too fucking comfortable with that bitch. I been calling your phone all day and you haven't been answering, but you're answering that bitch's phone?"

"Listen, Kiana, I'ma be real with you; I don't really want to be with you anymore. I have a baby on the way, and I wanna be with my baby mama."

"Aw, naw, homie, who did you ask?" I quickly hopped up. Homie was moving too fast. Kiana was right; Boss was getting too comfortable.

"You keep denying me for a bitch who keeps denying you. Boss, tell me how that works?"

"Shorty, you have one more time to call me a bitch."

"Or what?" she challenged.

"Say the word and find out."

"Bitch, bust your move. I'm outside your door."

Quickly hopping up, I charged toward my front door, but Boss grabbed me up before I could turn the doorknob. "Move, Boss. I want to fuck this bitch up," I yelled, trying to break free from his grip.

"You can want to beat her ass all you want, but that doesn't mean I'ma let the shit happen. Did you forget you're pregnant?"

"You're right," I said, backing away.

"I'll handle her." Boss sighed, relieved I wasn't about to go outside and show my ass, or so he thought.

"Boss, I wish you would think you're about to come out here, trying to check me over that bitch."

Moving in the opposite direction, I went in search of my purse. Finding it, I found what I was looking for inside before walking outside to find Kiana and Boss arguing. The moment Kiana spotted me, she tried to run up, and she wasn't alone. This bitch had the nerve to bring a vicious looking American bully with her. The dog was doing as much barking as its owner. The only difference was, I could tell his bite matched his bark, unlike Kiana's.

"Ask yourself if running up on me really a smart move on your end. The worst thing you could do is run up on a bitch like me. Your nigga didn't tell you I played with guns?" I asked her, pointing my gun at her.

"Baby!" Boss called out. I could hear him pleading with me. Boss knew what I was about, and sadly, he didn't think to warn his bitch.

"That's whore shit. Put the gun down and fight."

"Naw, girl. Now tell me why I would do that when I can lay a bitch down with a single shot." I smiled before putting a hole in between her dog's eyes, instantly lying her dog out.

"Princess! Get up, baby!" she cried out. I was an animal lover. I didn't go around killing dogs, but it was either them or me, and I chose them before this hating-ass bitch let the dog go to attack me.

"Your nigga knows better, so he should've taught you better. You see how you're crying over your baby? I will place that same pain and grief in your mother's heart if you keep fucking with me. Boss, get this bitch and her dog away from my house before I start letting shit fly. I'm here for the shits. I won't feel shit about taking both of you out and going on about my day." I slammed my door, locking it behind me. Walking over to the table, I grabbed Boss' keys and phone and quickly made my way back outside, throwing his shit out. I felt nothing about his phone crashing to the ground, shattering.

"Come on, Ro, you're on some bullshit."

"If I was on my bullshit, your bitch would be lying here dead, and not her dog. Get the fuck out of my yard before I change my mind." I shut and locked my door as Boss made his way toward me.

"Ro, open the fucking door." He banged as I made my way over to the couch, picking up my bowl of ice cream.

Picking up my phone, I called Ramsey. "Hello?"

"I'm doing everything in my power not to kill this bitch and our nigga," I spoke into the phone, taking a bite out of my ice cream. Boss was still banging on my door as if he had no home training.

"Not our nigga, Rory," Ramsey laughed.

"But he is, that bitch just needs to get with my program. Some days, I don't want that nigga to be my baby daddy, but most days, he's on his shit. Only if he could get this bitch in check."

"Is that him beating like that?" Ramsey asked, concerned.

"Yeah, I locked his stupid ass out. I just had to kill this bitch's dog. Shorty showed up confident as hell with her crazy-ass dog in tow. I humbled that bitch real quick, breaking that bitch's spirit with a bullet right between her dog's eyes. Rory never misses her target."

"Rory, you need help. You're crazy!" Ramsey cracked up on the other end of the phone.

"Not as crazy as Boss, talking about Kiana, I don't want to be with you. I have a baby on the way, and I want to be with my baby mama," I laughed. "That nigga is real deal crazy. Like, I'm confused at who told him that would be a good idea. I got to stop spending time with this nigga; I'm giving his ass false hope and shit."

"Rory, stop acting like you don't like Boss," she giggled.

"I do like him. Let me rephrase that; I like parts of him. His mouth and I have a love-hate relationship; the only time I love his mouth is when it's being really friendly with my lower lips, and his dick, well, he's my bestie." I laughed, happy the beating at my door had finally stopped.

"I don't see how he deals with your ass."

"Deal with me? I haven't caused that nigga nearly as many problems as he causes me. All I wanted from that nigga was him to nut in me so my baby and I could live happily ever after, but no, this nigga wants to be around, be a father and shit."

"Rory, you sound dumb as fuck."

"I feel dumb. This nigga won't let me be great. I was warming up to the idea of him being around, but this bitch Kiana is not about to work my nerves."

"Rory, that's her nigga."

"Correction, it was her nigga; now she occasionally shares him. I don't get why she's having trouble understanding that. Ramsey, you know me, I don't want any nigga. You know I'm phony as fuck. Most days, I just don't feel like being bothered, and when I do, that's when Boss becomes our nigga."

"You need help. I wish a bitch would tell me something about Zoo being 'our nigga'. I'm killing that bitch and him."

"I wish a bitch would tell you that shit, too, and you accept it. I'm beating your ass, hers and Zoo's."

"How is this logic of thinking acceptable in your book and eyes, but if the roles were reversed, motherfuckers would end up dead?" Ramsey laughed.

"Simple, that's just not the role I'm willing to play. My man is my man. If I ever choose to take Boss serious, I'm going to let him know having other women besides me is unacceptable. Nigga, if you feel the need to see other people, I have no problem switching it up. I already been thinking about dabbling in wearing wigs anyways."

"Rory, I seriously think we need to give you a psych evaluation." Ramsey cracked up laughing.

"I'm not crazy, just dead ass."

"That's the sad part."

"Whatever, I'm getting sleepy. Are you free for lunch tomorrow?" I asked, yawning.

"I'll let you know if I can make it. Zoo's been acting like I'm delicate since finding out I'm pregnant with triplets."

"As expected. If you can't make it, I'll just come over, and we'll have Zoo's ass go out and get us some food."

"Sounds like a plan. Love you, sister. Don't be over there killing people," Ramsey giggled.

"I can't make any promises, but I'll try not to. Have bond money just in case."

"Bye, crazy."

Cleaning up my mess in the living room, I made my way upstairs to my room to take a nap. This was the one thing I hated about being pregnant; I wasn't used to my body being tired and constantly shutting down on me. I had a feeling I would be sleeping the rest of my day away.

∾

RAMSEY and I had just left Outback on a sister date, and I had filled her in on Boss calling and texting me all day and night. I was convinced his ass was crazy. The text started off nice with him apologizing and explaining how he was done with Kiana and she was just having a hard time getting the picture. I felt like their ass were just alike because he had a hard time getting the picture of me not wanting to be with him as well. It didn't take long for Boss to start with the threats. One of the texts said my face wasn't pregnant, so when he saw me, he was going to smack the shit out of me. I laughed it off before making sure my gun had enough bullets. The day he smacked me would be the same day he met his almighty maker. He called over twenty times and sent about the same amount of threatening text messages. I paid Boss no mind because, in my eyes, he was nothing to me.

"How's Lulu been doing?" I asked Ramsey as we rode down the street. I wasn't about to spend my day thinking about Boss.

"Luna has no clue she was in danger, so she's been fine. You know Nanna called me this morning saying Jen keeps calling her, but she didn't want to tell me and get me upset. Your evil little sister had the nerve to call our grandmother and ask her to send money."

"I hope you're fucking joking."

"No, her dumb ass even asked Nanna if she could look out for Lance as well."

"This bitch is going to make me commit a petty crime, so I can come see her ass."

"You and me both. Zoo said he would get Boss to put a block on Nanna's phone, and get a better security system for her house."

"Why Boss?" I rolled my eyes.

"Because that's what he does for a living," Ramsey laughed. "Boss is damn near a genius when it comes to technology. Hacking, security, hell, anything tech is his specialty. He has a legal business, but he also does his own thing on the side as well. Rory, do y'all have conversations about life?" she asked, laughing.

"Bitch, no! Why don't y'all understand I only use that nigga for dick!" I mean mugged her.

"What the fuck?" Ramsey quickly swerved and hit the brake; she didn't want to hit the car that had pulled over in the middle of the intersection.

I was angry and confused until I watched Boss hop out, charging in the direction of Ramsey's car like a raging bull.

"Rory, get the fuck out the car," he yelled, banging on the passenger side window. I calmly reached into my purse, making sure I had my baby, "Bella Banger".

"Boss, your ass better stop banging on my shit!" Ramsey yelled, pissed.

"Fuck all that, Ramsey, unlock the door!" he yelled while people honked their horns because we were holding up traffic.

"Back up a little bit, and I'll gladly get out."

Stepping back a little, Boss allowed me enough room to open the door and step out. He was right back on my ass the moment I was fully out the car. Jerking me up, he yelled in my face. "So, you didn't see me calling and fucking texting you?"

I smirked because this nigga thought he was crazy. Little did he know, I didn't quite have it all. I moved so quickly, he didn't see the blow coming his way until it was too late, and my gun crashed into his face, slitting his shit wide open.

"Uh, shit!" Boss yelled, taking a few steps back, holding the gash above his eye, hoping that would stop the blood from running down his face.

"Fuck you thought this was?" I asked before throwing my gun on the floor of Ramsey's car. "Do I look like Kiana, nigga?" I asked, walking up on him. When I was close up on him, I started swinging.

"Fuck him up, Ro!" Ramsey yelled from the car. "Beating on my damn window. My man just got me this damn car, destructive-ass nigga."

"What possessed your dumb ass to pull over in ongoing traffic in front of two pregnant women?" I wildly hit Boss anywhere. "Did you think about your child or your nephews? Clearly not, or your dumb ass would've thought of a different approach! What if Ramsey would have run into your dumb ass, huh?" I was so pissed.

"Ro, stop fucking hitting me!" Boss barked, trying to back away, but I was on his ass."

"Naw, bitch, you wanted a huge scene, so, bitch, you got action!"

"Ro, what the fuck I say!" he said, roughly grabbing me up by my hair.

"Boss, let her go!" Ramsey yelled.

"Naw, Rah, keep the same energy you just had! Hype this shit up. Come on, hype me up, Rah. Tell me to fuck her up. Come on, Rah, coach me like you was just coaching Ro!" he yelled, dragging me by my hair over to his car.

"Let my hair go. Ramsey, grab my gun and shoot his ass," I yelled, pissed I didn't have it on me.

"I done told your stupid ass about playing with that gun!" Boss let my hair go to roughly grab my face.

"But who's playing? I guess you took me busting your shit open ass a joke. That's funny because I don't see you laughing!"

"You carrying my baby is the only thing sparing your nutty ass right now." I could tell he was beyond pissed right now, but so was I. "Get your nutty ass in the car and drive me to the hospital," he said, opening the driver side door for me.

"Dumb-ass nigga, I bet you didn't see this ending with you making a trip to the hospital." I laughed before getting in the driver seat.

"Shut your ass up."

"You shut up and walk your stupid ass over there and get my gun and purse." I didn't give a fuck about him bleeding.

"Ramsey, I'll call you later." I smiled, blowing my sister a kiss. "Boston, hurry up and get your dumb ass in the car before I leave you out here bleeding."

After Boss hopped into the passenger side, I quickly pulled off, making my way to the hospital. Everything in me wanted to drop his ass off at the curb of the emergency room and keep it moving.

"You're begging for me to kill your ass." I cut my eyes from the road to look over at him.

"Trust me, the feeling is mutual. Right now, I'm thinking of all the ways I could murk your ass after you have my baby." He was laid back with his eyes closed with his shirt pressed against his eye.

"Whatever, nigga. You keep up the dumb shit, and you're not going to make it that far." When I didn't get a smart remark back, I looked over at Boss because I was now at a red light.

"Boss, don't go to sleep," I called out, but got nothing. "Boss!" Still nothing. "Boston!" I yelled in a panic. "Baby, get up!" I shook him. Still nothing. Of course, I wanted to hurt his ass, but not kill him. "Boston, baby, wake up!" I gently slapped his cheeks several times once I pulled over to the side of the road. It was clear he had lost consciousness.

"Now you want to act scared." His words slurred. "Rory, get out of my fucking face and get me to the hospital. I'm dizzy as fuck."

"Try to keep your eyes open. Don't go to sleep." I pecked his lips.

"Ro, get your nutty ass out of my face," he said but kissed me back.

I guess I had hit Boss pretty hard because the whole way to the hospital, he went in and out of consciousness. I was quite amused listening to Boss lie to the doctor about what had happened to him. His pride wouldn't allow him to say he was pistol-whipped by his baby mama. I guess saying he wasn't paying attention and banged himself up sounded better. He was in this hospital, sounding like a battered woman lying to cover her abusive boyfriend's ass. Not only did Boss have a concussion, but he also had a blood clot in his eye and needed over ten stitches.

11

RAMSEY

I t had been a little over two months since the kidnapping, and I was skeptical about meeting up with Lance's other baby mama, Summers. Since my own sister had crossed me, I found it hard to trust people. There was no question about if her son belonged to Lance because he looked too much like my children, who looked just like their no-good ass daddy.

I had a talk with the twins about them having another brother besides the triplets, and surprisingly, they were excited. Seeing that they didn't want anything to do with Lance, I thought they would feel some type of way about having a brother. Luchi was extremely hyped about having another brother.

Today we were finally meet Summers and Journee, so the kids could finally meet. I didn't know if Summers had any hidden motives besides the kids meeting, so I asked Crash if it was okay for me to invite them to Lil' C's birthday party at the trampoline park. Luna was running around with Lil' C and Cari while Luchi sat by my side, waiting for Summers and Journee to show up.

"Is everything good, baby?" Zoo asked, walking over to me.

"Yeah, I'm good." I tugged on his shirt, pulling him down to my eye level so I could kiss his lips. We had to remember we were at a kid's party.

"That's why your ass is pregnant now." Luchi shook his head, and Zoo smacked him in the back of his head, causing me to laugh.

"Aye, homie, keep your hands off my brother," a voice said, grabbing our attention.

"Journee, no!" Summers looked embarrassed at her son. Zoo chuckled.

"He's good, bro. I'll let you know if we need to jump him. Daddy, you can thank me later for saving your life," Luchi joked, jumping at Zoo like he was going to hit him.

"Really?" Zoo asked, amused. "You've had a brother for all of a few seconds, and now you want to switch up on a nigga?"

"You're damn right," Luchi cheesed proudly. Journee and Summers' eyes grew big once they heard the curse word leave Luchi's mouth.

"Luchi, language." Zoo smacked him again. It was now my turn to look embarrassed. Luchi gave us both a look like whatever.

"Let me properly introduce everyone. Luchi, this is your brother, Journee and his mother, Summers. Journee and Summers, I'm Ramsey, this is my boyfriend, Zouk, and your sister Luna is bouncing around here somewhere," I said, looking around to see if I could spot Luna.

"Come on, bro, I'll introduce you to her."

"Is that okay, Ma?" Journee asked Summers.

"Yes, go have fun," Summers smiled. After getting the okay, Luchi and Journee ran off, and an awkward silence grew between us.

"I'll let y'all talk." Zoo kissed my lips twice before quickly walking off before I could stop him.

I didn't know what to expect with Summers. I had only had the conversation with her at the hospital, and we had texted a few times, arranging a meetup. For the sake of my kids, I promised to meet up with Summers with an open mind. Her attitude didn't come off as a bitter baby mama out to give the other baby mama hell; she seemed like she was all about her son and really wanted our kids to have a relationship. Although their daddy decided not to be in their lives, that didn't mean they couldn't be a part of each other's lives.

"So...," Summers awkwardly giggled.

"Right. Let's sit."

"I want to say thank you for what you did for my daughter."

"No problem. I have a feeling you would've done the same if the tables were turned; plus, I can't believe Lance and Nicki."

"You're shocked by Lance and Nicki's actions, just imagine how I feel about my own baby sister trying to play me. Not only was she sleeping with him, but she also orchestrated the whole damn thing."

"Yeah, that's really messed up." Summers seemed genuinely saddened to me.

"So, how old is Journee?" I asked, trying to change the subject to something lighter.

"He's eight. How old are the twins?" she asked.

"Eight as well. Their birthday is February sixth."

"You're joking, right? Only Lance's sorry ass." Summers let out a sarcastic laugh, shaking her head. "Journee's birthday is February fifth, and the crazy part about it, he came sliding out at 11:58, a few minutes before the clock hit midnight."

"You're telling me our kids are only a few hours apart?" I asked, shocked. Lance kept reaching different levels of pathetic for me.

"That's Lance's sorry ass for you. The only good thing that came from dealing with his ass was my son."

"I can agree with you on that one hundred percent."

"Oh, I have a present for the birthday boy," she said, raising the gift bag in the air.

"Come on, the gift table is over here." I slowly got up from my seat; my back was beginning to hurt.

Walking past Zoo, he smacked my ass, lustfully staring at me. I couldn't help blushing. After placing the gift on the table, we joined the table where the rest of the adults sat.

Summers sat next to Rory while I sat in Zoo's lap. "Everyone, this is Summers; she's the mother of the twins' brother, Journee," I announced.

Summers got a lot of what's up and heys from everyone.

I thought it was rude when I didn't hear her speak back, so I looked over at her, wondering what her problem was. A smile quickly spread across my face. Something, or should I say, someone, had Summers stuck. She didn't speak because Crash's brother Steel had her full attention.

"Aye, Steel, do you believe in love at first sight?" Rory asked, laughing. Steel smirked, and Summers' eyes lit up. She was really in a spell over him. It was no secret Summers had spaced completely out.

"Summers," I giggled, calling her name. "Summers!"

"Summers!" Steel called out.

"Yes, I do." She smiled at him, causing everyone to fall out laughing.

"Oh, my gosh," Summers cried out in embarrassment after realizing what she had said. "I'm about to go check on the kids." She quickly got up from her seat, rushing away.

"This nigga just got him a whole wife," Crash laughed.

"A bad one, I might add. Congrats, nigga," Boss laughed, checking Summers out as she walked away.

"This nigga loves to be knotted up and bruised." Rory smacked the back of Boss' head.

"Stop blocking, you're not my girl." Boss rubbed the back of his head, mean mugging Rory.

"I'm whatever I say I am, depending on how I feel in the moment. Right now, you better stop playing with me before you make another trip to the emergency room." She pointed her finger at Boss' face.

"I'm not going to keep telling you to watch how you talk to me." Boss smacked her hand away from his face.

"I'm about to go check up on Summers. Come on, Rory and Brad." I eased out of Zoo's lap. I wanted to stop Boss and Rory from turning Lil' C's birthday party into a WWF wrestling match.

"Ramsey, no bouncing around." Zoo grew serious.

"Yes, sir." I rolled my eyes.

Finding Summers, she had a sour look on her face.

"Please don't say y'all came over here to laugh at me some more," Summers whined.

"Brad and I didn't, but Rory probably did," I said, knowing my sister.

"Girl, where was your head at?" Brad laughed.

"At my damn wedding." She laughed as well. "I don't know what came over me, I heard you introduce me to everyone, but everything faded when I laid eyes on, what did you say his name was?"

"They call me Steel, but for you, my wife, you can call me by my government, Sergio," Steel said, grabbing our attention.

Embarrassment quickly washed over Summers' face again. "You know what comes after saying I do, right?" Steel asked Summers, intertwining their hands as he invaded her personal space.

"Ma, what's going on?" Journee asked, breaking up their little moment.

"Um, nothing, are you having fun?" Summers asked Journee, moving away from Steel.

"Yeah." Journee looked at Steel funny.

"Mama, you trying to jump with us?" Luchi asked.

"I would love to, but Daddy said no," I fake pouted.

"You already look like you're hurting. These kids are being wild as hell, plus I don't want to hear you complaining later about your body hurting." Zoo and Zay now joined us as we stood off to the side.

"Mama, I'm about to go get my sister so you can meet her," Journee said before bouncing away.

I smiled. Journee was so proud to call my kids his brother and sister. My smile quickly disappeared as I watched some little boy push my daughter down. Journee was the first to spring to action, coming to Luna's aid, pushing the little boy down while yelling at him. Luchi and Zoo weren't too far behind. What shocked me the most was Lil' C; he started fighting the little boy. Crash rushed over, pulling his son off the little boy.

I had never seen Lil' C so upset as Crash carried him away, kicking and screaming.

"Are you okay, Lulu?" I asked. Zoo was carrying her in his arms.

"Yeah, I'm perfectly fine." Her beautiful smile showed. I kissed her cheek before we made our way back into Lil' C's party room.

"Lil' C, good looking out. I'm glad my little baby has so many hitters looking out for her."

"It's my job to look after her; I'm going to marry her one day." Lil' C spoke seriously, catching Zoo and me off guard.

"Aye, Crash, check your peoples. Nine years old or not, I'll fuck his little ass up over my daughter."

"Daddy, he's always saying that stupid shit; that's why we stay getting into a fight." Luchi announced displaying the same mean mug as Zoo.

"Feel how you want, it's the truth. Someday, Luna will be the wife of Cordae Chambers Jr." Lil' C laughed, knowing he was torturing both Zoo and Luchi.

Looking over at Luna, I couldn't believe my eyes. Luna blushed, holding onto Lil' C's every word.

"Luna, you better fix your fucking face," Zoo spoke through clenched teeth. I could tell Zoo was seeing red, and sadly, I was quite amused.

"Seems like all my little niggas are finding love today. First, lil' bro, now my son's out here confessing his love. All these Chambers weddings are about to be popping," Crash joked, dapping up his brother and son.

"Luna, didn't Daddy say fix your fucking face? I'm confused at what you're over there smiling about? I'm about to fuck this nigga up." Luchi charged after Lil' C.

I laughed. "Luchi, stop!"

Lil' C ran around the table, laughing, trying to get away from Luchi.

"Chill out, bro-in-law!" Lil' C tortured Luchi. This was Lil' C and Luchi's normal behavior, and now I understood why.

Journee blocked Lil' C, causing Luchi to catch him.

"So, y'all just going to jump me." Lil' C laughed, amused as Luchi and Journee tackled him to the ground.

I was shocked to see Luna jump down from Zoo's lap, running to

Lil' C's aid, fighting her brothers. "Get off him." Luna laughed, putting Luchi in a chokehold.

"That's right, lil' baby," Lil' C laughed. Journee had him in a chokehold as well.

"I'm about to beat this little nigga's ass my-damn-self." Zoo mean mugged Lil' C. I could tell he was serious about every word.

"Let my little nigga be great," Crash cracked.

"It's all fun and games until I really beat his little ass."

"Relax, Zoo, he's only a kid. He's only joking," I laughed, trying to reason with him.

"Y'all see me laughing, but I'm dead serious," Lil' C cracked.

Ba'Cari entered the room, not knowing what was going on, but he jumped right into the mess, helping Lil' C and Luna.

"Back up, baby, Cari got me." Lil' C continued to get under Zoo, Journee and Luchi's skin.

"Oh, I see what this is about. Bro, I keep telling you she's our cousin," Ba'Cari said, now switching sides, helping Journee and Luchi.

"And I keep telling y'all no, she's not my cousin. She will one day be my wife; hopefully, on her eighteenth birthday." Journee choked Lil' C, but he got his words out.

"Journee, let him go, now," Summers called out to him. Doing as he was told, Journee let him go. Luchi hopped right on Lil' C, choking him out.

"Enough, Luchi," I called out.

"Daddy?" Luchi looked at Zoo, waiting for his approval.

"Daddy your ass, let him go, now!"

"Daddy?" Luchi called out again.

"Boy, I will beat your ass." I quickly got up to go over to him.

"Luchi, let him go, and Rah, sit your ass down." Doing what Zoo said, Luchi let Lil' C go.

"Come here, Luchi." I didn't like how he felt he didn't need to listen to me.

"I'm about to go jump."

"Get over here, now! If I have to get up, you're not going to like it."

"By the time you get up and make it over here to me, I'll be gone," Luchi said before running out of the room.

I cut my eyes at Zoo, pissed. Since finding out I was pregnant with triplets, Zoo babied me, and Luchi tried my patience, undermining my authority. I was already ready to have these babies.

12

BRADLEIGH

I loved living with Zay and Ba'Cari. I got to see the stand-up man Zay was and how awesome Ba'Cari was, and the amazing young man he was growing up to be. I loved how they welcomed me in with open arms with no judgment.

Zay took care of all my needs if I wanted him to or not. I didn't want to seem like I was only around just to mooch, so I tried my best to do my part around the house. I made sure a hot meal was on the stove every morning and night, and I cleaned and did laundry. School started about a month ago, and I didn't want to overdo it by taking on too much, so I only enrolled in two classes so I could have enough energy to come home and take care of Ba'Cari. I loved helping him with his homework. After we did homework and ate dinner, I would spend an hour with him before bed working on his artwork. We both shared a love for art.

Today was no different. I was leaving my last class and heading to the grocery store to get the rest of my dinner for tonight. I was in the mood for turkey and dressing, so I started cooking my meal last night. Zay had allowed me to use one of his three cars, so I had no problem getting around. After getting everything I needed to complete my dinner, I decided to pick Ba'Cari up from school early.

Pulling up in the garage, I saw that Zay was home as well. Normally, he worked at the shop until closing. I guess he was in the kitchen and heard the garage door open because he was now standing in the doorway.

"What's up?" he greeted us the moment we stepped out of the car.

"Hey, Zay." I faintly smiled before focusing on the bags in the back seat. I didn't mean to be rude, I was hungry. If Zay wanted to talk, he could do so while I moved around the kitchen, cooking.

"Move, you know better than that," Zay said, gently moving me out the way as he grabbed the grocery bags from Kroger.

Shaking my head, I smiled. You would think my hands were made out of glass the way these two fussed over me. Zay loved to tell me to play my role whenever I tried to take the trash out, move something heavy or carry things.

"What's up, dad?" Ba'Cari said, grabbing some bags. That was one thing I loved about this kid; he didn't have to be told to do things. He knew what Zay expected from him, so he did so.

"What's good, son? You're home early." Zay looked at his watch.

Nervousness washed over me. I knew Zay didn't play about Ba'Cari's education, so I hoped he didn't feel like I was overstepping by picking him up without his permission.

"Um, I'm sorry, I just decided to pick him up since I was already by his school."

"You're good. I decided to cut my day short as well to spend time with y'all."

"Okay, well, I'm about to finish up dinner."

"Ba'Cari, go wash up, and I'll help you with your homework."

"Okay, my homework is to create a solar system."

"Why are you just now saying something? Now we have to run out to get everything you need."

"I have everything I need. Brad took me to the store the other day." Cari smiled over at me.

I tried not to overthink the way Zay was staring at me. I was trying to control my feelings from growing stronger for him, yet it was difficult. I had his baby growing inside of me, and watching him be a father to Cari tugged at my heart. I wanted that bond and relationship he had with Cari for my baby.

"Go change, and we can get started." Doing as he was told, Cari rushed out the kitchen to change his uniform.

"Do you need help with anything?" Zay stood behind me.

"No, I got this under control."

"How does a little girl know how to burn like this in the kitchen?"

"Don't call me that, I'm not a little girl," I snapped.

"Brad, just because you have a belly don't mean you're not a baby. You're just a lil' baby having a baby." He pinched my cheek like he often did to his eight-year-old niece, Luna.

I slapped his hand away, frustrated. I didn't want him to see me as a little girl. One day, I had to tell him the truth about me carrying his baby, and sadly, I was hoping the four of us could be a family.

"Look at your little attitude, it's kind of cute."

"Zay, just leave me be and go help Cari." I slightly pushed him away from me. I was getting annoyed by him using words like little girl, describing me as cute and calling me a baby.

Zay laughed, exiting the kitchen. Counting to ten, I tried to get my anger and frustration under control. Today my attitude was off; I found myself ready to snap over the simplest things. I rolled my eyes at Zay when he entered the kitchen, causing him to laugh.

After putting my macaroni and sweet potatoes in the oven, I joined them at the kitchen table to help build Cari's model. I quickly lost my little attitude. Zay wasn't having it anyway; he went out of his way to make sure Cari and I were always smiling. We sat at the table for a few hours, building the model while joking and laughing.

The doorbell rang just as I was getting up to check the food. "I got it," I said, stopping Zay from getting up from the kitchen table.

Walking to the door, I looked through the peephole to see who it was ringing the doorbell like crazy. Seeing that it was Angel on the other side, I rolled my eyes before opening the door.

Pushing past me, she walked past me as if I didn't exist. I really couldn't stand her. Locking the door, I made my way back into the kitchen.

"Really? So y'all in here having family time and nobody thought to call or text me to tell me not to pick up Ba'Cari from school?"

"That's my fault, I apologize. I was over by his school, so I decided to pick him up early." I apologized because I understood why she was upset.

"So, since when did you get the authority to start making decisions around here? It's becoming really clear you're gunning for my spot."

"And what spot is that, Auntie? What is the real problem, auntie?" I asked. I tried my best to keep the peace between Angel and me, but every time she was in my presence, she made that difficult with her slick mouth and jealous ways.

Hearing Zay chuckle pissed her off. "I got your Auntie, young bitch."

"Aye, Angel, chill out." Zay continued to laugh.

"You stay trying to check me, check her ass. She stays in the wrong, but somehow, shit always gets turned around on me."

"Cari, go to your room for a second. Let me take care of Angel, and I'll call you back down to eat dinner and finish up."

"What do you mean, after you take care of me? Zay, you've really been showing your ass since this little bitch been around," Angel yelled.

"Angel, you know I don't put my hands on females, but if you don't lower your voice, I'ma show you something," Zay spoke through clenched teeth.

I continued to move around the kitchen. I was hungry, and I wasn't about to let Angel stop me from what I was doing. I rolled my eyes when the waterworks started. This was becoming normal when it came to Angel, and this was how she got Zay to kiss her ass.

"Za'Cari, I'm so tired of this," she cried harder.

"Tired of what, man?"

"I'm the pregnant one. Hell, one would think I would be the overly emotional mess running around here," I spoke under my breath.

"See, that!" she yelled, pointing at me. "She can say and do what she wants, but the moment I speak up for myself, you talk to me like I ain't shit."

"Oh, my!" I laughed. She stayed starting shit, yet her ass stayed playing the victim.

"You excused Ba'Cari from the kitchen, you should've excused her ass as well. She has a problem with staying in a child's place," Angel spoke to Zay.

"No, you're the one who has a problem staying in your place. You're the nanny, Auntie, but you stomp through here like your last name is Taylor. You knock to get your access granted in here, so act like it," I said before checking my food in the oven. I normally didn't feed into Angel's negativity, but today, I had time. I was already crabby and in a mood.

"I'm about sick of your presence." Angel tried to rush me, but Zay grabbed her.

"Aye, Angel, have you lost your fucking mind?" Zay roughly pushed her back. "You really been violating lately. You stay coming in here, disrespecting my son, my house and my guest. Did you really just try to put your hands on her? Angel, you're real deal bugging the fuck out. You need to get out of my shit right now."

"You know what, Zay? Fuck you. When it's all said and done, you always choose her. I quit, and I quit you."

"Bye. Your services were no longer needed anyway." I politely smiled, knowing that would get under her skin.

"Brad, chill, because if she tries you again, she's going to get more than a rough push."

"What's with you and this stray?"

"Bitch, I got your stray," I said, getting worked up. Although Zay had given me a place to stay, the reality was, if Zay kicked me out today, I would be back to square one. I was still homeless.

"You want to keep letting me know I'm the nanny. Bitch, you work around the house for room and board," Angel laughed. "You're working overtime to earn your keep around here."

"And you said all that to still be threatened by my presence. I thought you quit; why are you still here?" I said before storming out of the kitchen. Angel's goal was to get under my skin, and she did the job; she hit the mark right on the bullseye. I stormed up to my room; Angel had killed my whole mood and appetite.

I moved around my room, slamming things for no reason. I never hated anyone in my life as much as I hated Angel.

"Brad, you don't have to worry about Angel anymore."

"Whatever, Za'Cari." I rolled my eyes before turning my back to him.

"What the fuck are you mad at me for?"

"I'm not, I just want to be left alone."

"Well, too fucking bad. You live with two other people, so that's kind of impossible. You cooked us a dinner, so come downstairs and eat."

"I'm no longer hungry."

"Well, you're about to eat regardless for the sake of the baby. Stop acting silly, Bradleigh."

"I'll eat later."

"You'll eat now," Zay said, grabbing my hand, pulling me out of my bedroom.

I pouted as we made our way down the stairs and back into the kitchen. I wasn't in the mood to eat.

"Sit down, I'll make the plates," Zay said, guiding me over to my seat at the kitchen table.

"Look at me." Zay placed his finger under my chin, turning me to face him. "Bradleigh, fuck everything she said. If I got it, so do you. We're a team now. As long as you take care of the home front, I will always provide your every need, so stop tripping over dumb shit people say. Our understanding is the only thing that matters. Continue to hold my son and me down, and I'll do the same for y'all." Zay placed his hand on my stomach, rubbing my belly. "Do you understand?" His words were comforting, yet I was still pissed, so I kept quiet.

"Bradleigh, do you understand?" He stared deeply into my eyes, waiting for me to answer.

"I hear you, Zay." I rolled my eyes, breaking our intense stare down.

"Hearing and understanding are two different things. Do you understand I got you and the baby no matter what a motherfucker has to say? You stay looking out for Ba'Cari and me, so I'll always look out for you." He was now sitting on the table in front of me, rubbing my belly in circular motions.

"I understand." I hated how I held on to Zay's every word any time he spoke.

"Good, now let's eat." He kissed my forehead twice before kissing my nose twice.

"Ba'Cari, let's eat!" Zay yelled out for Cari.

"I'm right here. What are y'all in here doing?" Ba'Cari smirked suspiciously.

"Mind yours, young one, and let's eat. I'm going out tonight with Crash to get a few drinks."

"Cari, we can have movie night before bed."

"Sounds like a plan."

I WAS EXHAUSTED TRYING to carry Ba'Cari's heavy self to his room. Zay was out at the club, so tonight, Cari and I had a movie night in my room. It was going on three in the morning, and I couldn't get comfortable in my bed, seeing that I was five and a half months pregnant, making it difficult for me to get any rest. After getting Ba'Cari comfortable in his bed, I made my way downstairs. I was going to the kitchen to get a late-night snack before making my way into the living room to get comfortable in my new massage chair Zay had bought me.

Getting myself a pickle and some plain Lay's potato chips covered in hot sauce, I made my way into the living room. The living room was pitch black, but I knew my way around pretty well, so I moved around without bumping into anything.

Placing my bowl of chips and pickle on the table, I felt around for the remote on the coffee table so I could watch a little TV. After finding it, I plopped down in my massage chair.

"Ahhhh!" I screamed, trying to hop up. From my understanding, Ba'Cari and I were the only ones home.

"Chill, lil' mama, it's just me," Zay announced, tightening his grip on my waist.

"Oh my gosh, Za'Cari, you frightened me."

"My bad." He stood to his feet with me still in his arms. Turning me around to face him, Zay sat back down with me straddling his lap.

"How has your night been?" Zay asked, pulling my shirt up over my growing belly.

"We ate junk food and watched movies; you know, the normal," I said, trying to control my nervousness as he rubbed my belly in circular motions.

"Cari didn't give you any trouble, did he?" he asked in between placing kisses on my belly.

My nerves were getting the best of me, and I needed to get away from him. I tried to move out of his lap.

"I'm not done talking to you," Zay spoke, so close to my lips, I felt his lips brush up against mine with each word he spoke. I could also smell the liquor on his breath. I should've known he was drunk because he was being so touchy.

"Cari never gives me problems, Zay," I whined. I was ready to go hide in my room.

"That's good." It was dark, so he caught me by surprise when his lips touched mine.

I didn't want to, but I couldn't help kissing him back. Our lips felt like magnets connecting.

"Zay, what are you doing? You're drunk," I whined, breaking our kiss. I realized Zay had a habit of drinking so much, he often blacked out, not remembering anything he did while under the influence.

He ignored me as he gently pulled me close, kissing my neck passionately.

"Zay," I moaned.

"Damn, my name sounds so sweet rolling off your tongue." He

was now sucking on my neck. I was pretty sure I would have hickeys come tomorrow morning.

"Goodnight, Zay. It's time for me to call it a night." I quickly pulled away before he could stop me.

Zay was right on my heels as I made my way to my room. I stopped to check in on Ba'Cari first. I could feel Zay's hard dick pressed up against my ass as we looked in on Ba'Cari as he slept peacefully.

"Goodnight, Zay." I stopped in front of my bedroom door.

"Come on!" His voice was so gentle, yet so demanding as he placed my hand into his, guiding me up the hall to his room.

"No, Zay." My mouth said one thing, but my feet continued to move in the direction of his room.

"I just want to lay with you." He removed my shirt the moment his bedroom door shut.

"You can't lay next to me with clothes on?" I asked while he removed my pajama pants. I was now standing in the middle of his bedroom floor in my bra and panties set. After removing my clothes, he removed his.

"Yes, but I want you like this." Drunk Zay was different from sober Zay. Drunk Zay didn't give me much of an option when it came to most matters. He was very demanding, yet his gentle heart always shined through.

Pulling the cover back, he helped me get up on his king size bed. He pulled me close to him the moment he got comfortable.

"You good?" he asked, fluffing the pillow behind my back.

"Yeah."

"Good." He smiled before kissing my lips, then leaning down to kiss my belly. I choked back tears. Zay showed genuine love for my baby, not knowing she was, in fact, a part of him as well. I was so caught up in feeling guilty, I didn't notice Zay was no longer next to me; he had disappeared under the cover, and his juicy lips were now sucking on my lower lips.

Pulling the cover back, I tried to push his head away. "Zay, stop, you don't know what you're doing. You're drunk."

"Does it feel like I don't know what I'm doing?" he asked, flicking his tongue faster against my clit, causing me to push his head deeper into my wetness.

I was having flashbacks of the night we had spent together. I knew this was wrong, yet it felt so right. I'd been feening for his touch since I walked out the hotel room that night.

"Zay, please stop, we shouldn't cross this line," I moaned. I didn't really mean anything I was saying.

"Baby, I'm not turning back now; this shit is too sweet." He was talking, yet never missed a beat of making me feel good with his tongue. He sucked and licked until my body shook uncontrollably.

Zay wasted no time attacking my neck, sucking on my spot while he played with my nipples. They were sensitive to his touch. The way he sucked my neck and played with my nipples had my juices flowing.

"We can't do this," I protested.

"Why not?" he asked.

"Because you're drunk, and you really don't know what you're doing when you're drinking."

"Bradleigh, I know exactly what I'm doing. I just ate your pussy, now I'm about to make love to your body."

"Zay!"

"Chill, baby." He covered his lips with mine while rubbing my clit.

I got so caught up in our make-out session, I was caught off guard by Zay pushing himself inside me. I moaned out in pleasure. Oh, how I missed the feeling of him being inside me.

"Are you okay? Am I hurting the baby?" Zay stopped all movement, looking down at me, concerned.

"Yes, I'm more than fine," I moaned into his mouth, taking his bottom lip into my mouth, biting down on it.

"Let me know if I'm hurting you, baby." He kissed my lips before staring deeply into my eyes. Muscles rippled throughout his body as he positioned himself to keep his weight off my body. I cried out in pleasure as he teased me with different series of moves and strokes.

"Zay!" I cried out as I felt his teeth latch on to my neck. He was teasing me, thrusting halfway in and out, teasing me with only the tip of his dick. Removing his dick, he stroked up and down the outside. Reaching down, I grabbed his shaft, rubbing it against my clit until I reached my second orgasm.

Flipping me over to my side, he wrapped my right leg around his waist, which gave him easy access to enter me. This sex position allowed me to lay comfortably while Zay deeply thrust in and out of me. I almost lost my mind when Zay also started rubbing my clitoris, bringing me to another mind-blowing orgasm. I didn't know how much more I could take, but from the way Zay flipped me into a different position, I knew our night wasn't ending anytime soon.

I SNUCK out of Zay's room this morning before he or Ba'Cari could notice. After quickly showering and dressing, I stopped by Krispy Kreme Donuts to get us breakfast before dropping Ba'Cari off at school. When I got back home after dropping Ba'Cari off, I peeked into Zay's room, and he was still knocked out. After checking on Zay, I made my way back to my room. I didn't know when it happened, but I fell asleep. I was now up, thanks to my alarm clock beeping, alerting me that I needed to pick up Ba'Cari.

"Rise and shine, sleeping beauty." I was greeted by Zay the moment I walked into the kitchen. He was grabbing a donut from the box I had sat on the counter this morning.

"Hey." I avoided eye contact with him.

"If you're still tired, I can go pick up Ba'Cari."

"It's no problem, I got it." I was trying to get away from him, but my body was betraying me, feening for his touch.

"Why are you so short? I know you're not still mad about that shit with Angel."

"No, Zay, I'm not worried about that. I'm okay."

"Aye, what the fuck you do last night after you and Cari's movie night?" His change of tone caught me off guard.

"What?" I asked.

"Fuck you mean, what? Did you have company last night while I was gone?"

"No, Za'Cari!"

"So, you left my son here by himself?"

"Zay, what are you talking about?" I asked, genuinely confused.

"What am I talking about?" he yelled, pacing the floor. I didn't understand his rage. Grabbing a bottle of water from the fridge, I made my way out the kitchen.

"Where are you going?"

"Where do you think? To pick Ba'Cari up from school. I don't know why you're tripping."

"You don't know why I'm tripping?" He let out a sarcastic laugh. "Look at your fucking neck." He roughly grabbed me up. He was now all in my face, trying to get a better look at my neck. "This is what I'm talking about. This shit wasn't there when I left yesterday."

"Zay, you need to chill out." I snatched away from this crazy fool.

"I'm not doing shit until you explain yourself to me. How did your neck get like this?" He backed me up against the wall.

"You need to stop drinking, Zay. It's clear you have a problem."

"My only problem right now is you and this shit on your neck."

"Za'Cari, get out of my face." I forcefully pushed him back. "I'm going to pick up Cari from school, then I'm going to hang out with Ramsey, Rory, and Summers; I'm taking Cari with me. We'll be back later." I made my exit, not giving a damn about the death stares he shot my way.

I was frustrated because I had no one to talk to about what was going on between Zay and me without revealing my dark secrets.

13

RORY

I was floating on cloud nine. Boss and I were on a high after leaving our doctor's appointment, finding out the sex of our baby. I was over the moon to find out we were having a baby boy.

We were now out, having a late celebration lunch. Ramsey wanted to throw me a gender reveal party like the one I had thrown her, but I was too excited to wait.

"Baby, since you told me we were finding out the sex of the baby, I've been thinking of baby names." Boss' smile melted my heart. My heart was doing things I didn't want it to do, pissing me off. I smiled over at him. I had tried so hard not to love this man, but moments like this is what made it so hard.

"What did you come up with?"

"I won't tell you the girl names because it's not important now since we know we're having a little nigga."

"Let's not start with that little nigga shit. You mean our young king? What boy names did you come up with?"

"I was thinking Boston Jr." He caressed his full beard in a cocky manner.

"Fuck nah, nigga!" I laughed, cutting him off. "Your mammy was dead wrong for naming you that. What the fuck I look like punishing my son with that terrible-ass name?"

"Man, you're disrespectful as fuck." Boss laughed, shaking his head.

"What else you got? What other names do you have on your list?"

"Rory, I refuse to let your ass boss up on me when it comes to naming my son. I'm going to pick his name, and you're going to like it."

"Talk all you want, but if I don't like it, it's not happening." I playfully rolled my eyes before taking a bite of my burger.

"Our son's name is Brody, like it or not." I found the nervous look on his face cute.

"Brody?" I asked, hiding any emotion in my voice.

"Yes, Brody."

"I like it," I giggled. I loved giving Boss a hard time.

"Good." He leaned over the table to give me a kiss. The passion behind the kiss had me forgetting we were in a crowded restaurant.

"Nigga, are you really out here showing this bitch public affection like you don't have a whole girlfriend?"

"Not today, Satan," I whispered, pulling away from Boss.

"Kiana, what the fuck are you doing here?" Boss asked, frustrated with her presence.

"Boston, don't question me when it's your ass that's in the wrong," she yelled, grabbing the attention of others sitting around, trying to enjoy their lunch. I continue to eat my food, paying her ass no mind.

"You didn't see me calling you?" She continued to yell like it was needed, like her ass wasn't all up in Boss' face.

"I didn't answer because I told your ass what the fuck I had going on today. You knew we had a doctor's appointment to find out the sex of our baby. You need to move from around here, you're interrupting our celebration lunch."

"You got me out here going crazy, putting tracking devices in your car and shit. Nigga, fuck your celebration lunch!" she yelled, smacking my burger out of my hand right as I went to take another bite.

"Bitch!" I quickly hopped up from my seat, smacking the shit out of her. That bitch said and did a lot of shit I allowed her to get away with, only giving her a good cursing out, but playing with my food was a major hell no. She deserved these hands, pregnant or not.

"I've been waiting for that." She cocked her arm back, ready to strike. Catching her arm, Boss gave me an opening to punch her in the face.

"Are y'all really trying to jump me?" Kiana dramatically screamed. She was really swinging her arms wildly, trying to get away from Boss. Boss was calm for the most part until Kiana brought her foot up to kick me in my stomach. Grabbing her up by the neck, neither Kiana nor I saw it coming.

"Bitch, are you out of your fucking mind? Behind my girl and son, I will do time. Bitch, you're real deal out here violating. I will choke the life out of you and happily do my jail time." The wild look in Boss' eyes and the chill in his tone let everyone around know he was more than serious. I didn't feel sorry for this bitch, not one bit, but I didn't want Boss behind bars, so I decided to call him off. "Come on, baby, let's go before the police arrive."

Squeezing tightly one last time, Boss let her neck go. "On my son, Kiana, stay the fuck away from my girl and me. I have been telling your ass for months I don't want to be with you anymore. You better get that shit through your head before you lose your life." Boss shot Kiana a murderous look before throwing money on the table for our meal. Grabbing my hand, he ushered me out the restaurant. I was pissed people had their phones out, recording this shit.

We weren't in the car good, and Boss' phone was going off like crazy. I could put all my money in my bank account on it being Kiana on the other end of his phone. Boss helped me into the car before jogging around to get in himself. By now, he had the phone to his ear, causing me to roll my eyes.

"Kiana, man, I'm not trying to hear that shit. I almost killed your dumb ass because you wanted to be on some stupid shit and not play your role," he said, placing his phone on speaker before starting up the car.

"Boston, how could you treat me like this?" she cried. "You want me to play second to her when I was here first. I am your woman, and I should be the mother of your child."

I rolled my eyes. What she was saying held some truth, yet I didn't sympathize with her.

"You tell me to play my role, and I am. My anger is valid, my hurt is valid. I've done nothing but love you over the last few years, and one night changed our whole life. Our good outweighed our bad, and that means nothing to you. What does she have that I don't?" Kiana screamed into the phone.

"My son," he said before hanging up with her. The ride back to my house was a silent one. I had a lot on my mind, and the way Boss constantly let out frustrating sighs, it was clear he was second guessing how he felt, and Kiana's words were affecting him. My anger was starting to get the best of me. I talked my shit, I was slightly in denial, but truly, I had feelings for Boss. If I was being completely honest, I was excited about the thought of us being a family. For months now, Boss had been trying to convince me it was best we be together, but my stubbornness always pushed me away from the idea.

I didn't notice we had made it back to my house until I felt Boss' hand grab mine to help me out the car. I let him help me out but quickly snatched away once I was safely out the car.

"Rory, don't start with your bullshit as well," Boss said the moment we stepped foot in the door.

"Boss, don't compare me to that bitch."

"Well, you and Kiana act just alike, always fucking bitching and nagging me."

"I haven't said shit to your ass! If you don't like the shit I'm saying right now, you can walk right out the door the same way you walked through it. I can see how you're second-guessing me and my child, just remember I never asked you to be here, so stop making shit so hard for yourself. Go home to your bitch," I yelled. I wanted to break down and cry, but I refused to come off weak to this nigga.

"You know what, you damn right about that; I should be at home with my girl. Every day I'm over here damn near begging your ass to be with me when I can be at home with my girl, a bitch who wants to be with me, who wants to build a family with me! All you do is give me a hard fucking time."

"Bye, leave, what the fuck is stopping you?" I screamed. I didn't want to break down, but my emotions got the best of me.

"You're what's stopping me! Despite you constantly pushing me away, I want to be with your ass. I want to raise my son in a two-parent household surrounded by love. My love for you is what's stopping me from always smacking you in your smartass mouth. I don't want to be with no other bitch, and you know you don't want me to be with no other bitch, so stop with your constant bullshit before you write a check your ass can't cash," Boss said before storming out of my house.

Grabbing my keys and purse, I rushed back out the door. I was going to Ramsey's house. I ran into Boss on the way out. "Fuck you running off to?"

"I was going to talk to my sister." I tried to push past him.

"That's your problem. You run around here wanting to talk to everyone but me." Boss dragged me back inside.

"You stormed out of here, so I figured you were going home to be with your woman."

"You're my woman, you're carrying my son. I love you, and I want to be with you, all I want you to do is let me in."

This was the first time Boss had told me he loved me. He swept me right off my feet like I was light as a feather, and his lips crashed into mine. I knew how we would spend the rest of our day once I saw him head up the stairs.

14

Bradleigh

UNTITLED

Zay and I were in a weird space since he had flipped out about seeing the hickeys he had made on my neck. I wasn't going to tell him he had made them because he shouldn't get so pissy drunk to the point where he couldn't remember what was going on around him. That night was a small dent in a huge problem we had.

My birthday is tomorrow, and I was excited because I was turning eighteen. I wasn't surrounded by blood family, but the one I was building with Zay was so much better. Tomorrow, Zay was throwing me a birthday dinner, so I was out doing some shopping with the girls. It was an elegant dinner, so I wanted the girls to help me find something grown and sexy.

"Bradleigh, I told you weeks ago to order your damn birthday outfit online. Got us strolling through the mall, looking like the damn baby mamas club. I'm surprised Zoo let Ramsey come. I'm pissed she thought it was okay to ride around this damn mall in this Hoveround." Rory looked at her sister, embarrassed.

"Shut up, Rory. This was the only way Zoo would allow me to come with y'all."

"Where the hell did Zoo get a Hoveround anyways?" Summers laughed.

"Hell if I know. I'm ready to have these babies so he can get off my back," Ramsey pouted.

"We only have two more months to go."

"Lucky bitches. I pray my four months fly by." Rory rolled her eyes.

"Thank God, for birth control. Steel been trying to trap my ass. Not happening."

"Aw, naw, bitch. Tell that nigga it's too soon." Rory rolled her eyes with a look of disgust on her face.

"Says the bitch who purposely got pregnant on the first night she met a nigga. Rory, take your judgmental ass on somewhere." Ramsey mean mugged Rory.

Summers and I giggled. Ramsey was right; the nerve of Rory. Rory had told me the story about how she had gotten pregnant on one of our many late-night conversations on the phone. Hearing her crazy story made me want to confess mine, but I wasn't as brave as Rory.

"Oh yeah, I forgot I did that," Rory giggled, rubbing her belly.

I'd gained so much these last couple months, my girls being one of them. Thanks to them, I was breaking out of my shell and becoming the person I was once afraid of being.

It was difficult getting any shopping done, thanks to each of us stopping throughout the mall, purchasing food. I had a craving for cinnamon buns and ice cream, and Ramsey and Rory wanted popcorn and pretzels. We also stopped at the food court to grab some Chick-fil-A. After eating, we finally made our way to Dillard's.

After an hour of searching, I finally found a beautiful, red sequined, lace, long sleeve gown with a pair of red Steven Madden pumps. After leaving the mall, we went to the nail salon for manis and pedis. I wanted to get my dreads freshly done but decided to rock a wig instead. I was excited about my birthday dinner.

～

I danced around in the passenger seat as Zay pulled into Ruth's Chris. Looking out the rear window, I watched as everyone pulled in behind us here to celebrate me. Zay showed out, making my birthday special. We were now about to enter Ruth's Chris to attend my private birthday dinner.

I almost cried; the setup was beautiful. Red balloons decorated the room. Standing by the big one and eight balloons, I asked Summers to take a picture. The moment I posed, Zay walked into my picture. I looked at him lustfully, checking out his attire. He looked so sexy in his suit, tattoos and all; Zay could pull off any look.

Zay stood behind me, wrapping his arms around my waist. "Y'all look so cute together," Summers beamed.

Zay had been real possessive since our fight over the "mystery" hickeys. "We're not together," I smiled, pulling away after Summers took the picture.

Walking away, I went to find my seat. I had on heels, and at almost eight months pregnant, I didn't want to overdo it with too much standing.

"Where are you going?" Zay asked, grabbing my hand, stopping me from walking away.

"I was going to sit by Rory."

"Nah, you're going to sit right here next to me," he said, pulling my seat out.

I wanted to put up a fight. I didn't want to cause a scene and come off ungrateful, so I took a seat next to Zay. I looked around the table at my new family and friends. Everyone was coupled up, looking beautiful and handsome. "I would like to thank everyone for coming out and celebrating my birthday with me. I looked around the table, making eye contact with everyone sitting amongst me. Rory swore up and down she and Boss aren't anything special, yet yesterday, she was picking him out an outfit that matched hers, just like the rest of us. They looked like bosses in their blue, and they were dripping with diamonds. Summers and Steel rocked all black. They looked like the perfect couple. Crash and his date weren't matching, yet they were equally fly. Pregnant and all, Ramsey looked amazing, and when my eyes landed on Zoo, the look he was giving me was frightening. It was as if he hated me.

I tried to smile at him, but that didn't work. The look he was giving me was as if I was his worst enemy and he wanted to rip my head off. Looking away, I focused my attention on Zay.

"Thank you so much, Za'Cari, I really appreciate this."

"No problem, baby. Happy birthday." I was caught off guard by him pecking my lips. "Did I mention how beautiful you look?" he said, resting his hand on the side of my neck before pulling me closer to him.

"Thank you."

"Can I have a kiss? A real one?" he asked.

"What's got into you?" I asked, blushing, running my hand down the side of his face. I loved the way he looked at me.

"You!" He leaned forward, kissing my lips. I moaned as he slid his tongue into my mouth.

"If y'all wanted to have a moment, why invite us?" Rory asked.

"Ro, shut up and get out their business," Boss checked her.

"You're right, why am I tripping? Have all the moments you need. Sometimes my mouth blocks my blessings. Bitch, relax, why are you tripping off getting a free meal?" she said, talking to herself. I giggled, something was truly off about Rory.

"I'll be looking into getting you checked out." Ramsey shook her head at her sister.

My attention was pulled away from Rory and Ramsey as the waiters began to bring everyone's food out.

"No wait time, happy birthday to me." I danced around in my seat as the waiter placed food in front of me.

"No way was I coming out to a group dinner with three pregnant women without ordering ahead."

"Smart man." I licked my lips at all the food being placed on the table.

Jumbo shrimp, barbecue shrimp, and crab cakes were placed in front of Ramsey, who sat next to me. Steakhouse salad, creamed spinach, sweet potato casserole, asparagus, and potatoes au gratin were also placed on the table before the waiters started passing out everyone's main dish. Placed in front of me were filet and twin lobster tails. Zay's plate housed a delicious looking ribeye.

Conversations flowed as everyone enjoyed their meal. I was enjoying the great conversations and great laughs, but the way Zoo kept staring at me had me sitting uneasily.

This little girl was sitting on my bladder, so I excused myself to go to the ladies' room. After using the bathroom, I took a minute to get myself together. Something was telling me Zoo and I had an underlining beef, and that was something I didn't want. After washing my hands, I exited the bathroom.

"I know you," Zoo called out from behind me, stopping me in my tracks.

"Huh?" I asked, confused.

"I said I know you."

"Of course, you do, silly." I laughed nervously.

"Nah, like, I know who you are. The devil in the red dress," Zoo spoke, walking around me in a circle. It was like he was finally seeing me for the first time.

"Excuse me?" I asked nervously, my palms instantly beginning to sweat.

"I knew your ass looked familiar. I was drunk as fuck that night, but seeing you all dolled up like this, I remembered. You are shorty from my birthday."

I didn't say anything, just stood there trying to get my poker face together. Zoo's rude attitude already scared me, and now he had discovered my secret.

"You left with Zay the night of my birthday, correct?" Zoo asked. His tone let me know it was a rhetorical question. He already knew the answer to his own question, but he wanted to hear me say it anyway.

"Yes."

"April was about seven months ago, right? Now, how far along are you again?" Zoo asked. By the knowing look on his face, this was another rhetorical question he knew the answer to. My tears began to fall; I couldn't find the right words.

"You don't have anything to say?" he asked. "It's okay, I'll do the math. So, when did Zay meet you in the park?" he asked sarcastically. "It was in the middle of July, and you were about four months pregnant, right?" Still, I said nothing.

"April, May, June, July." Zoo put up a finger with each month he called out. "July! That's four months after my birthday, four months after the night you left the club with my brother."

"Listen, Zoo," I said, finally finding my voice. "I wasn't expecting to run into Zay that night at the park."

"But you did, and you've lived with him for a little over three months, and you have yet to say anything."

"I've wanted to, I just don't know how."

"Well, you better figure it out. You have twenty-four hours to speak up before I do."

"Zoo, please!" I broke down.

"Sorry, Brad. I don't give a fuck about none of that; he has the right to know."

My birthday started off so well, but now things were quickly falling apart. With Zoo knowing my truth, I knew I had to come clean. Everyone continued to enjoy themselves while I sat uncomfortably in my seat, waiting for this dinner to be over.

Zay kept asking me what was wrong, and I forced a smile, not ready to come clean at this very moment. Zoo's intense staring throughout the remainder of the dinner didn't help any.

I was quiet the whole way home, trying to find the right time. I just couldn't. I had never been so terrified in my life. I felt like I had so much to lose, and I wasn't ready.

"Goodnight, Zay." I kicked my heels off the moment I entered the front door, leaving them there in the middle of the floor. I made my way up to my room.

"Wait, Brad, we need to talk." My heart stopped, thinking Zoo had said something to Zay.

"Can it wait until tomorrow, Za'Cari? I'm tired."

Ignoring me, Zay pulled me into his room, and my eyes lit up.

Candles were lit, and balloons, roses, and rose petals decorated his room.

"Zay, what is this?" I wiped my falling tears.

"Bradleigh, what does it look like?" He wrapped his arms around my waist from the back. "Happy birthday again, baby." He kissed my neck before unzipping my dress. I couldn't blame Zay's affection on his drinking tonight because he barely had anything to drink.

"Did you enjoy yourself tonight?" he asked, grabbing my hand, ushering me into his connecting bathroom.

"Yes, thank you, Zay."

"Your night isn't over yet." He kissed my cheek before pushing the bathroom door open.

Roses and candles were everywhere, and the tub was filled with red and white rose petals. The white rose petals were beautifully shaped into a heart.

"I thought you would like to relax after dinner, so I had this setup," he said, helping me into the bathtub. I moaned as I felt the hot water against my body.

"Would you like to join me?" I nervously asked. I wanted to be close to him, not knowing what tomorrow might bring.

I watched as he removed his clothes. This man was everything to me, and there was a possibility I would lose him. Rising, I let him ease in behind me. Wrapping his arms around me, Zay placed his hands on my belly.

"Your wig is getting wet," he laughed, tugging on the end. "You can take it off now."

"Shut up, don't act like you don't like it. You've been in my face all night."

"I just want to make you feel special on your day."

"Well, you did a good job. Tonight was great."

"A nigga's tired. I'm ready to lay in bed with you."

"Who said I was doing all that?" I smiled, looking over my shoulder at him. Of course, if he asked, I would lay next to him.

"Stop fronting." He grabbed my face, bringing my lips to his.

"I want to be with you," Zay spoke, breaking our kiss.

Tears fell from my eyes. This was everything I wanted, and I saw it quickly slipping away.

"I'm ready to go to bed." Getting out the tub, I walked over to the shower. Exiting the tub, Zay joined me.

"You don't feel the same?" Zay asked, turning me to face him.

"Of course, I do, but..." I tried to stop the tears from falling.

"No buts, why are you crying?"

"Nothing, Zay, I'm just tired. Can we go to bed, please?"

"Yeah," he said before washing me up.

I tried to sleep on the edge of the bed, but Zay wasn't having that. Pulling me close, he kissed my forehead, nose, and lips several times before closing his eyes. I watched him sleep, wondering how things would've been if I started off our relationship with the truth. Kissing his lips, I closed my eyes, dreading tomorrow.

BRADLEIGH

Zoo had given me twenty-four hours to come clean to Zay, and my time was now up. I didn't have it in me, so I was packing up me and my daughter's things to get out of dodge. I knew running wasn't the answer, I just needed time to get my thoughts together.

I'd been planning my escape since being confronted by Zoo last night at my birthday dinner. This morning, Zay dropped Cari off at his parents' house to give me a break while he went to work. Getting my day started, I cleaned the house, did laundry, cooked and quickly packed our things. I even left a bottle of Henny and two pre-rolled blunts waiting on Zay. This was the first time I wanted him to drink and smoke until he forgot I was missing.

I hoped Zay wasn't crazy enough to call the police because I was taking his car with me. I also had his credit card that he had given me the other day to go shopping for my birthday outfit with. I was going to use it to check myself into a hotel until I figured out my next move. Driving downtown, I grabbed a bite to eat before checking into the Seelbach hotel. I'd stayed at this hotel before with my parents, so I knew I would be comfortable staying here. I had to give the girl at the front desk a sad story and a couple hundred dollars for her to swipe Zay's credit card without his ID.

I decided to leave all our belongings in the car, only bringing in my overnight bag so I could shower. After eating and showering, I climbed into bed, exhausted from cooking, cleaning, and packing; I was ready to call it a night. I was debating if I wanted to turn my ringer off or not. I knew Zay was home from work right now and had realized me and all my things were gone. Just when I decided to turn my ringer off was best, a FaceTime call from Zay came through.

I didn't want to talk to him on FaceTime because I didn't want him to see where I was. Ending the call, I called him back by audio.

"Hello?" I spoke, the moment he answered.

"I just tried to call you on FaceTime, why didn't you answer?"

"I have a poor connection," I lied.

"Aye, Brad, where you at, man?" Zay yelled into the phone.

"Listen, Za'Cari, I want to thank you for helping me get on my feet, but I'm okay now. I found a place."

"So, this the thanks you give? You just up and move out without giving a nigga a heads up?"

"I'm sorry, Zay, it was just time for me to move on."

"Oh, really? You're just going to leave my son's life without so much as a goodbye? I told you I wanted to be with you last night, so it's fuck that, too, huh?"

"Zay, it's not like that."

"So, tell me what it is, Brad. I come home to find all your and the baby's shit packed and gone."

"Zay, I've been wanting to tell you everything," I cried.

"Tell me everything like what, Brad? Stop fucking speaking in riddles."

"Zay, I just don't know how to explain." I cried.

"Explain what, Bradleigh? I feel fucking used right now."

I didn't know how to explain the situation without sounding crazy. The situation was so messed up, I didn't know if I should just blurt it out or explain everything to him from the beginning.

"Zay, you're my child's father!" I blurted out.

The line went silent. Looking at the phone, I realized Zay had hung up on me. "Oh my goodness," I cried harder.

I finally had the balls to tell him the truth, and it didn't go how I planned.

To calm my nerves, I decided to soak in this amazing bathtub in my hotel room.

ZAY

"Yo, I'm about to kill this little bitch," I yelled, calling Boss' phone.

"Yo!" he answered on the fourth ring.

"Aye, yo, Boss, do you think you can find Brad for me? I need her location in the next thirty minutes. I came home to find her and all the baby's shit gone. She got me fucked up, and that's not even the fucked-up part. She's on some mind games, speaking in riddles and shit, talking about I'm her baby's daddy. I need you to find her so I can fuck her up." I yelled at him like he was the cause of my problems.

"I got you, bro," he said before hanging up the phone.

Hearing a knock at the door, I rushed to it, hoping it was Brad's dumb ass. I pulled the door open, ready to flip out on her, only to find my brother standing there.

"Fuck you want?" I yelled, taking my anger out on him.

"Bitch, what's your problem?" Zoo's attitude matched mine.

"I came home to find Bradleigh and all her shit gone. I'm going to kill her ass once I find her. She got me fucked up." I paced back and forth, waiting for Boss to call back.

"I came home, and she cleaned everything out; no trace of her or the baby. I never wanted to beat a bitch's ass as much as I want to put my hands on Bradleigh right now."

"Have you talked to her?"

"Yeah, she cried into the phone, talking about she didn't know how to explain to me why she left. She's tripping hard and talking crazy. She was talking about I'm her baby's father. I hung up on her ass and called Boss to find her. I don't know what the fuck she's on, but I'm about to find her ass and beat some sense into her," I said just as my phone began to ring.

"What did you find, Boss?" I asked, placing him on speakerphone

"She's at the Seelbach Hilton on the Fourth Street. It didn't take me long to find her because she used your credit card to book the room. She got the bed and breakfast package for a week, and that shit ran you one thousand, six hundred and forty-three dollars, plus two hundred and sixty-four dollars and three cents in taxes, leaving the grand total of Bradleigh's week stay at Seelbach Hilton, one thousand, nine hundred and seven dollars and three cents." Boss laughed like shit was funny.

"Yeah, I'm about to beat her ass. Good looking, Boss," I said before ending the call.

"Zoo, lock up on your way out."

"Nigga, I'm riding," he said, following me out the door.

"Good, you might have to stop me from strangling this bitch until she's blue in the face."

"Yeah, I already know shit's about to get real," Zoo said, giving me a knowing look.

I bitched the whole way to the hotel. I was looking forward to coming home to Bradleigh, so just imagine how pissed I was to come home to a silent, empty house, only smelling the nice aroma of food I normally came home to after a long day of work. Not only was I going to beat her ass for leaving, but I was also going to try to kill her ass for packing and carrying everything out of my house at almost eight months pregnant.

Storming into the hotel with Zoo hot on my heels, I walked up to the front desk. "Welcome to the Seelbach." The young girl behind the counter smiled up at me.

"I need access to Bradleigh Lambert's room."

"I'm sorry, sir, that's against hotel policy to give out customer information."

"Was it against hotel policy to swipe my fucking credit card for two fucking grand without my damn permission?" I asked, ready to smack this bitch. The look on her face said it all.

"Listen, sir, relax. I don't want to lose my job."

"Give me what I want, and I'll be out of your hair."

Typing away on her computer, she looked up Bradleigh's information before giving me all access to Bradleigh's room.

My anger rose with each floor level we rode the elevator up to Bradleigh's floor. Hearing the elevator ding, we walked off the elevator.

"Chill, bro, remember she's pregnant."

"Naw, she should've remembered she was pregnant before she packed and lifted heavy boxes and shit."

"Bro, I get that you're mad, and you been doing a lot of threatening, just know I'm not about to let you go in here and put your hands on this girl, so get your temper under control." Zoo stopped me as I was about to let myself into Bradleigh's hotel room.

"Man, watch the fuck out." I pushed him out the way.

Walking into the room, it pissed me off how nice it was. I didn't want her pregnant, living out of a hotel, I wanted her at home with Ba'Cari and me. "Bradleigh," I called out, walking through the hotel room. I found her sitting in bed with a shocked look on her face.

"Zay, how did you find me?"

"Brad, it wasn't that hard to find you, considering you used my credit card."

"What are you doing here?"

"Man, stop asking dumb-ass questions when I should be asking you that dumb shit. Get up and get your shit. You're seven months pregnant; you're not about to be living out of a hotel room. If that was a fucking option, I would've offered that to you the night I met you in the park!" I yelled.

"That's the thing, the park is not the first time you met me," Bradleigh screamed back as tears fell from her eyes.

"Brad, what the fuck are you talking about?"

"I met you before the park, Za'Cari, four months prior, to be exact," she said, avoiding eye contact.

"Do you remember anything from the night of my birthday party?" Zoo asked.

"Naw, man." I was confused. I didn't understand why he was making this about him when Bradleigh and I were trying to have a serious conversation.

"Za'Cari, this baby I'm carrying is your daughter," Bradleigh cried.

"Man, that's not possible."

"It's possible, bro. The night of my birthday, Bradleigh's young ass was in the club, playing grown, and you left the club with her, but I'll let her do the explaining," Zoo said, taking a seat in a chair.

The look on my face said it all. I was confused. "Explain, now!" I yelled, causing her to jump.

"It was never my intention to leave the club with anyone that night. I just wanted to break free from my parents' strict rules for one night, so I stole my sister's ID. I just wanted to get out, have a drink and enjoy music with my friend, Bonnie, and then there was you. I wasn't in the club, playing grown." She cut her eyes at Zoo. "I was in the club, just minding my own business, and you were all over me."

"Devil in the red dress is what you called her," Zoo butted in. "Your little devil. You were right about that because, for three months, she has been deceiving you," Zoo chuckled.

"Shut up, Zouk!" Bradleigh yelled, frustrated, but not as frustrated as me.

"Don't get mad at me, you little devil you!" Zoo laughed. I didn't take this shit as a joke.

"You know my story. I was a church girl just looking for a night of fun and got pregnant my first time having sex. That night you asked me to take you home, and I agreed, but before you could give me directions to your house, you passed out, so I took you to a hotel. I went up with you to the room to change my clothes so I could sneak into my house and one thing led to another and you took my virginity."

"You tricked me? I'm taking virginity from seventeen-year-old little girls out here trying to prove a point to Mommy and Daddy?" I yelled angrily.

"I didn't trick you!" she yelled back.

"I'm a twenty-seven-year-old grown-ass man, and I fucked a seventeen-year-old minor and got her pregnant; how the fuck does this look and sound?"

"You never asked my age," she cried, I guess hoping that would justify her actions.

"If I met a bitch in a twenty-one and older club, I wouldn't think I would have to. It's clear you can't be trusted, and now you want me to believe some shit I can't even remember. You could be making this shit up. You see I'm a good nigga, and you want to pin this baby on me, but I'm not buying it."

"Oh, so it's my fault that you are a fucking alcoholic and you drink to the point of blacking out?" she screamed. I hated to see the tears run down her face, but right now, it was fuck her and her feelings. None of this shit made sense to me. "Zay, the club ain't the only time we fucked. I guess I tricked you this last time as well, too, huh? You wanna know where the hickeys on my neck came from? Those were the results of another one of your blackouts," she screamed. We both looked like raging bulls.

"Brad, you're not the person I thought you were. I've dealt with a lot of crazy bitches in my day, but you have to be the craziest because none of them have made up some crazy-ass story like this."

"Fuck you, Za'Cari! I'm not making this up!"

"Bro, she's not lying. I was fucked up that night, but not as fucked up as you. Do I think her young ass was wrong for being in a club, acting like someone she's not? Yes, but it's true, you were all over her. You also told me you had plans to leave with her that night. She wasn't thinking about you, so you went looking for her. I watched y'all leave the club together.

"When I first met Bradleigh at your house after you moved her in, there was something about her that was familiar, I just couldn't place it. The girl we met at the club that night didn't have dreads, and that's why I never put two and two together until last night at Bradleigh's eighteenth birthday dinner. She had dressed up like the devil in the red dress again, and that was when it clicked. The next morning after my birthday party, you were still pretty fucked up when I picked you up from the hotel, and you turned around and got fucked up all over again that night, so that weekend was a little fussy for you. I did the math, bro; that's your little one she's carrying. The shit just adds up," Zoo explained.

Fire danced around in my eyes. Zoo must have known my next move because he grabbed me before I could leap across the bed and put hands on Bradleigh. Everything in me wanted to fuck her ass up.

The trust I had for this girl was shattered. "Bitch, you been living under my roof for three months, acting like a fucking stranger, pretending like the night in the park was our first encounter. All this shit is starting to make sense to me now. I remember the way you looked at me that night in the park. Never once did you think to tell me what the fuck was real? You're one sick-ass bitch, you know that, right, Bradleigh? Where is my fucking credit card? This room is already paid up for you, so you have a week to figure out your next move. I'm done with your ass. When you go into labor, that is when you contact me. I'm not claiming shit until I get a blood test done."

Zoo reached out to retrieve my card from her. "Zay, please, I never meant to hurt you, I was just afraid. I love you and Car. I didn't know how to tell you because I didn't want to lose you." I could hear the hurt and pain in her voice, but fuck her feelings. Out the door I walked as if I hadn't heard her talking to me. My fucking mind was blown. I had never been so damn confused about life as I was right now. I needed a fucking blunt or two.

BRADLEIGH

I was shocked to see Zay and Zoo walk through my hotel room door, but then again, I wasn't. I knew Zay wouldn't let me just leave without giving him an explanation. I didn't have high expectation when it came to telling Zay the truth; I knew he would flip out and feel some type of way. What I didn't expect was the high level of disrespect he had shown me. Did he have the right to question my character? Yes, but I felt like he couldn't place all the blame on me.

For hours, I had been sitting in the same spot since Zoo and Zay had left, crying my eyes out. I was so hurt by the way Zay had spoken to me. When it came to me, he didn't allow disrespect, so to hear it coming from him broke my heart in two. The way he called me bitches with venom dripping from his voice echoed in my head.

Although my main concern should've been that I was back at square one, pregnant and homeless, I couldn't help breaking down because I felt like I had lost my whole world when Za'Cari told me he was done with me. When I told him I loved him, I meant it. Yes, I loved him for everything he'd done for me over the three months I lived with him, but I was also in love with the man he was. This was my first time feeling heartbreak, and I felt like my heart was about to explode out of my chest.

Turning all the lights out in my hotel room, I welcomed the darkness. I had a splitting migraine, and I wanted nothing more than to fall asleep and wake up tomorrow morning and realize the last seven months of my life was all a big nightmare. False hope was what helped me doze off to sleep.

Two hours later, I was jumping up from a nightmare. Looking over at the nightstand, the clock read 4:30 a.m. It didn't take long before the tears began to fall again. Resting my head back on my pillow, I thought of the dream I had just had. I had given birth to a beautiful baby girl; my baby was the perfect blend of Zay and I. My beautiful dream turned into a nightmare when I had to watch Angel live happily ever after with what I felt was mine: Ba'Cari, Zay, and my daughter. That heifer cuddled my beautiful baby girl lovingly in her arms as if she had birthed her. I woke from my sleep as Zay leaned over to kiss her.

Feeling the sweat trickle down my breasts, I threw the cover off my body before getting out of bed. Stripping out of my clothes, I was in need of another bath. Walking into the bathroom, I turned on the shower. Reflecting on the last seven months of my life, I realized how one night had turned my whole life into a shit show. I wanted to feel regret for letting my parents down and feel guilty for misleading Zay, but I couldn't. I loved and wanted my daughter too much to allow anyone to make me feel bad about her existence. I was afraid to lose Zay, but I couldn't say if I were put in this situation all over again I wouldn't handle it the same way.

Exiting the bathroom after showering, I was shocked to see someone sitting on my bed. Turning the lamp on, Zay's face was now visible. I was happy to see that he had come back, yet nervous at the same time. I didn't know where his head was, and it was clear by how low his eyes were that he was high.

I didn't want to be the first to speak, so I continued to put my night clothes on in silence. Climbing into bed, I watched him bury his face in his hands. I could tell he was stressed. Nervously, I climbed to the edge of the bed where he sat. Wrapping my arms around him, I kissed the back of his neck as tears began to fall from my eyes again. "I'm sorry, Zay. I promise there were so many times I wanted to tell you, I was just too afraid of your reaction. How things happened was so crazy. After I realized you didn't recognize me the night at the park, I had no clue how I would tell you you got me pregnant from a one night stand you didn't even remember."

Snatching away, Zay walked out of the hotel room, causing me to lose it all over again. I didn't know what to say or do to make things better. The more I tried to explain, the madder he got. Turning the light back out, I curled under the covers, feeling completely defeated. I didn't understand why he had come back.

Feeling the bed dip, I peeked from underneath the covers. I stared at Zay, unable to read his facial expression as he intensively stared back at me. Taking his shirt and shoes off, he laid down next to me. I let out a sigh of relief when his head hit the pillow.

I flinched when his hand came close to my face. "Man, stop playing," he said, sucking his teeth. "Trust me, I wanna kill your ass right now, but I would never hurt you." He wiped my tears away with his thumb.

"So, if you hate me so much, why did you come back here?"

"Same shit I've been trying to figure out. I don't know why I'm here. Everything you said to me is a whole lot of bullshit, and I for damn sure don't trust you. You got me second guessing everything you've said."

I didn't want to lose Zay, so I had to be real with him; I didn't like the way he was looking at me right now. "Za'Cari, when I said I loved you and Ba'Cari, I meant it. Please don't question that. Please try to understand where I'm coming from. I was seventeen, fresh out of high school, trying to live a little. My whole life consisted of church twenty-four seven. I just wanted one night of freedom. Did I plan for that night to end with me in a hotel room, having a one-night stand, losing my virginity to a stranger? No. I'd been on edge since that night. Would my parents notice I walked differently? The guilt I felt for breaking my pledge. I hated myself for often fantasizing about that night with you. I walked across the graduation stage, knowing it was a new beginning, a new chapter. What I didn't know was the new chapter would begin with a baby. I was a preacher's kid, the poster child for bright girls with bright futures, and I was pregnant at seventeen by a complete stranger, whose real name I didn't even know. I had to hide and pretend like my life wasn't changing. I knew I couldn't hide this forever, and I thought I was prepared, but I wasn't. I was seventeen and homeless.

"When I saw you again in the park, I had mixed emotions. My first thought was you were kidding about not knowing who I was, and that's the reason I walked away. I got in your car that night because I believe in fate. I just wanted to feel you out some more. I noticed your heart the moment you handed me your jacket. After you opened your home up to me, everything began to move so fast. Like I said, I fell in love with you and your son, and I was afraid to speak up because I didn't want what's happening now to happen. I never wanted you to look at me the way you do now. I didn't want your tone to house so much anger when you spoke to me. There's no good way this could've been done. I at least thought that after you got to know me, when shit did hit the fan, you wouldn't question my character."

"If Zoo had never put two and two together, what would you have done? When would you have told me your so-called truth?" he asked.

"You really think I would lie about you being the father of my child?"

"Yes, I do think you would pretend like I fathered your baby. You pretended like you didn't know me." He raised his voice.

"Za'Cari, you can't play both sides." I sat up in bed, screaming. "Don't pick and choose what you want to believe about my story."

"Lower your fucking voice, and calm the fuck down." He placed his hand on my belly, moving his hand around in circular motions. Rolling my eyes, I smacked his hand away. He gave me a look while placing his hand back on my belly. "I told you already about doing all that screaming; don't stress her out."

"What do you care? She's not your concern until you get the blood test, right?" I smacked his hand away again.

"She's been my concern! I've been taking care of her and you, but I'm not about to go around claiming she's my flesh and blood until I get a test, period. You're still nothing more than the pregnant chick who I took in," he spoke, breaking my heart. I refused to let him see the effect his words had on me, so I turned over before the tears fell. I was done talking about it.

I silently cried until I dozed back off to sleep. Sadly, although Zay was giving me his ass to kiss, I felt at peace lying next to him. Feeling his hand rest on my belly while I slept gave me hope that he would come around and lose his attitude. Waking up the next morning, I rolled over to find Zay gone. Reaching for my phone on the nightstand, my hand ran across some money. Picking it up, I counted out fifteen hundred dollars before placing it back on the nightstand.

Dialing Zay's number, I waited for him to answer. "Hello?"

"What hospital you at?" Zay asked.

"I'm not."

"So, why are you calling me?" Zay's attitude was still the same from last night.

"Zay."

"Brad, we don't have shit to talk about. Contact me when you go into labor." He hung up before I could say anything else. Placing my phone back on the nightstand, I grabbed the pillow beside me, hugging it tight; it smelled just like him. Only day two, and I missed Ba' Cari and Zay like crazy. I was praying this wouldn't go on for the next few months of my pregnancy.

15

BRADLEIGH

For the last few weeks, I had been staying with Rory. I hadn't seen much of Zay, and the last time I talked to him was when I had called his phone the day after everything had hit the fan. I wasn't about to play myself by calling him when it was clear he didn't want to be bothered with me. Ba'Cari, on the other hand, I saw a lot. I was glad Zay wasn't being petty and keeping him away from me.

I wasn't for sure if he knew what was going on, but I doubt Zay had said anything, considering he said he wasn't claiming my baby until he got a blood test.

I allowed myself to have a pity party for two days before I pulled myself from the hotel bed and put my plan in motion. I had been kicked out of two places I called home within the last seven months. Needing to make money, I took the money Zay gave me and invested it all into new art supplies. For the last few weeks, I had been making money by selling my paintings, and I was doing pretty well. I had reached out to a few of the members of my daddy's church who loved and wanted to buy my work. My mother and father never believed in my art, so selling it under their roof was out of the question.

I appreciated Rory allowing me to stay with her, but I planned to be in my own place by the time my baby entered this world, which was in less than two months. I didn't want any more handouts. Although Za'Cari was still in his feelings, he made sure I didn't go without. Every other week, Rory was handing me fifteen hundred dollars. I would offer her rent, but she would decline so I would put the money away. Next week, I planned to go apartment hunting. I wanted to be in my own place and settled before the baby was born.

I was going to put all my worries to the side because today was Ramsey and my baby shower. I wasn't too excited. Although everyone welcomed me with open arms, this was Zay's family, and I didn't want to be one of those chicks who forced a situation or a baby on a man. The moment I found out I was pregnant, I was prepared to raise my baby on my own, and that hadn't changed.

It was the middle of November, so I dressed in a pink maternity dress and brown cowboy boots. I styled my dreads in a high bun. My baby weight I had put on had me looking older than eighteen.

"Why don't you seem excited?" Rory asked, looking from the road for a split second to look at me.

"Because I'm not. Times like this, I miss my family. This shows me how lonely I am. I really do appreciate y'all doing this for me, but I feel like it's out of pity because I have no family."

"Bitch, shut up. We are your family, and this shower is just as much for you as it is for Ramsey, so stop thinking like that and smile, we're here," she said, pulling up to this beautiful house I guess where the baby shower was being held.

Boss was waiting outside to help Rory with her baby shower gifts. "What's up, ladies? Y'all look beautiful," Boss said, hugging us both.

"Thanks." I smiled.

Walking into the house, we were greeted by a big, pink and blue banner that read, "Taylor Gang."

"Brad!" Cari yelled. He was the first to greet me once I entered the house.

"Hey, Car!" I hugged him tightly. Looking around, I smiled. Everything was decorated beautifully in pink and blue.

"Hey, boo, you look beautiful," Ramsey said, wobbling over to me.

"As do you." I hugged her as best as I could, causing us both to giggle because our bellies were in the way.

"It looks so beautiful, Rory. You did a good job putting this together."

"This isn't my doing. I'm too tired to stay up to finish watching a thirty-minute TV show, let alone plan a baby shower."

"My little baby is so gorgeous." Zoe walked over to me, being his normal turned up self.

"Thanks, love. You look gorgeous as always."

"What's up, sis?" Zoo walked up as well, giving Rory and me a hug.

"Hey, Zoo!"

"Here, put this on," he said, handing Ramsey and I a sash. Looking at it, I smiled. The front read, "Mommy-to-be" and the back read, "Taylor Gang." Mine was pink, and Ramsey's was blue.

"You like mine, Brad?" Cari said, grabbing my attention. Looking down at him, he, too, had on a sash that read, "Brother-to-be". I didn't know how to react, so I smiled awkwardly, hugging him. Zoo and the twins had on one as well.

Ramsey saw how uncomfortable I was, so she grabbed my hand, giving me a reassuring smile.

"Let's go find a seat, my back is killing me," Ramsey said.

"Let me show y'all the way." Cari grabbed my other hand.

"Here, Aunt Rah, this seat is for you." Ba'Cari pointed to the chair with the blue seat cover. Above it was a sign that said, "Triple "Z" Taylor."

"This seat is for you and baby sis." Cari smiled proudly. The name above read, "Carlee-Zay Taylor." I felt so overwhelmed and confused.

I guess Ba'Cari didn't plan on leaving my side because he pulled up a seat.

"Do you like her name? Daddy said I could pick it. It took me a few weeks because I wanted her name to be perfect. Cari and Carlee," he beamed proudly.

"I like the name Carlee." I smiled as well; his smile was so contagious.

Looking around, smiling at everyone in attendance, I got nervous when my eyes landed on Zay. He was talking to Crash and Steel but stared directly at me. Breaking eye contact, I turned my focus back to Cari and realized he and Zay were matching from head to toe. They looked so handsome in their pink and white, long sleeve button up shirts. I was pretty sure Ba'Cari had picked out their outfits as well because it was more of his preppy style than Zay's. Their button-up shirts were tucked into white pants, revealing their brown Gucci belts.

Cutting my eyes at Zay again, he, too, had on a sash that said father-to-be. Feeling the tears, I quickly blinked them away before they could drop.

"Do you need anything?" Cari asked me.

"No, I'm fine. Thanks, babe."

"I'm going to get you something to drink anyway, just in case." Cari ran off before I could protest.

"Aye! Aye! Can I get everyone's attention," Zay called out. I missed the sound of his voice. I listened to what he had to say, but I refused to make eye contact. "Now that both guests of honors are here, we can get things started. I want to thank everyone for coming out to celebrate with us the new additions to the Taylor Gang. I want to especially thank Summers for helping me put everything together. I know I've been acting like a Dadzilla, as she would call me." He chuckled, also getting laughs out of the guests. "This was my first time planning a baby shower, so I hope everyone has a good time and enjoy yourselves. We really appreciate everyone for coming out to celebrate the life of my nephews and daughter." Hearing him claim my daughter, I finally had the balls to look at him. "Everyone, feel free to eat up, and afterward, we will get some baby shower games cracking." He was speaking to our guests but never took his eyes off me.

I had no clue Zay was the one throwing the baby shower; I was just told to show up. I had no clue he had talked to Ba'Cari about everything, and I was even more shocked to hear him claim my daughter. Zay hadn't talked to me, but it was clear he was talking about me, or at least about the baby.

"I know you said you didn't need anything, but I went ahead and made you a plate anyways," Ba'Cari said, carrying a plate and drink in his hand.

"Cari, you didn't have to do that."

"I know, I wanted to so you wouldn't have to get up."

"He's such a gentleman. Look at Luchi over there, stuffing his face," Ramsey said, shaking her head. "He isn't worth a damn," Ramsey laughed, joking.

"Rah, you ain't my girl. Aye, daddy, your shorty is hungry, like always," Luchi called out to Zoo before biting into his hot wing. I laughed because Luchi had no chill.

"And Zoo wants me to be excited about having three more of his rude ass." She playfully rolled her eyes. "I pray at least one turns out to be like Cari," she spoke, closing her eyes and crossing her fingers.

"Don't trip. I already got you covered," Zoo said, placing two plates in front of her with a little bit of everything on it.

"Mama Renee and Nanna did their thing, like always," Rory said, walking over to the table eating.

"Sorry, I'm late," a familiar voice I hadn't heard in months spoke from behind me.

"Shani!" I screamed, jumping up from my seat. I was so happy to see my sister.

"Oh, my goodness, Bradleigh, you look so beautiful," she cried.

"Shani, I've missed you." I hugged her tight. Despite my sister turning her back on me, I was truly happy to see her. It felt good to be around someone who had known me all my life.

"I've missed you, too."

"Everyone, this is my sister, Shani," I spoke proudly.

Everyone greeted her. "You can have my seat, beautiful." Cari offered his seat beside me to her.

"A little charmer," she smiled.

"I'm Ba'Cari, brother of the bump." He smiled, hugging me, rubbing my belly. I giggled, hugging him back. If no one loved me in this world, I knew Ba'Cari did.

"Nice to meet you, I'm Shani, auntie of the bump," she laughed.

"Nice to meet you. May I get you anything?" he asked.

"If you were a little older, I would want your hand in marriage; you're such a gentleman," Shani joked. "You're already a well put together young man; it's clear you're being raised right."

"Thank you," Zay and Ba'Cari spoke at the same time.

"Hi, you must be Zay. Thank you for inviting me." Shani extended her hand for him to shake.

"No problem. I knew Brad would want you here." He spoke about me as if I wasn't right in front of him. "Help yourself to something to eat and drink."

"Okay, thank you," she said before Zay excused himself. I hated being in his presence and not getting any of his attention.

"Is everything okay?" Shani asked, concerned.

"You're here, so it's perfect," I said, putting on my poker face. I could tell she wasn't buying it, but let it go.

After everyone ate, Zay announced it was time to play some baby shower games.

Zoe and Summers were now hosting the baby shower games, and the first one everyone played was guess the baby items in the baby bag. Zoe and Summers passed around two diaper bags, and everyone had to feel around inside the bags without looking and write down all the items they thought were inside the bags. Crazy Aunt True won. After that game, we played baby sketch artist, which everyone complained about not being fair, knowing I had this game in the bag. I won drawing the best picture of what I thought my daughter would look like, and Cari and Luchi won for the best picture of the triplets.

The next game, the guests had to guess the mothers-to-be belly measurements. Ramsey wasn't here for that game; she even went as far as cursing Zay, Zoe, and Summers out for even picking the game. I got where she was coming from. Some days I felt like a fat cow, and I was only carrying one baby, so I knew how she had to feel carrying three babies.

The next game was solely for Zay and Zoo, and it was now their turn to bitch like drama queens. Summers and Zoe had them bobbing for bottle nipples. Ramsey and the twins cheered Zoo on while Ba'Cari and I did the same for Zay. He still hadn't said a word to me, but at this point, I was having too much fun to care.

The last game was the baby price is right, which my sister won. After that, Ramsey and I opened the baby shower gifts. Zoo and the twins stood by her side, helping her open presents; all their excitement was on the same level. I wasn't expecting much, and I was shocked at how much everyone had shown out. Everyone showed my baby and the triplets so much love. It was so awkward sitting next to Zay, opening presents together. He was just as excited as I was about the beautiful gifts.

The party began to slow down, and most of the guests were gone. All the guys stuck around to clean up while the girls and I lounged around the living room. My sister stuck around to catch up. The twins, Journee and Lil'C were all gone with Nanna. They wanted Ba'Cari to come but, of course, Ba'Cari wanted to be stuck to my hip.

"Today was interesting." I playfully rolled my eyes.

"Right, talk about an elephant in a room," Rory laughed.

"I'm out of the loop, but I noticed something wasn't right as well," my sister said looking at me.

"Cari, do you want to go see if your dad and uncles need some help?" I looked down at him. He was lying in my lap.

"Okay, I see when I'm not wanted," he joked, leaving.

"Overall, I had a nice day," I smiled.

"Zay seems like a nice guy, and he did a great job planning everything." Shani smiled over at me.

"Okay, so I'm just going to say what everyone's thinking," Rory said before taking a bite out of her cake. "So, I thought this nigga wasn't going to claim the baby until he got a blood test? Is it me, or did he look like a proud papa today?"

"I'm glad someone addressed the elephant," Ramsey laughed.

"I was just as shocked when he called me last week, claiming he wanted to put together a baby shower. He damn near had everything already planned out, he just wanted me to go shopping with him for everything he needed," Summers said.

"Not claiming the baby? I didn't get that impression when he called me?" Shani said, confused.

"Shani, you pretty much know about everything that happened and how I ended up with a huge belly, but the part you missed is I ended up running into my baby's daddy at the park the night our parents kicked me out. Long story short, he was so drunk, he didn't remember that night at the club. He opened his home up to who he thought was a stranger, and not once in the three months I was living with him did I have the balls to mention he was my child's father. On my birthday, Zoo put two and two together, and let's say shit hit the fan and Zay hasn't talked to me since, so don't look at me for answers, I'm just as confused as y'all. I didn't even know he had a conversation with Ba'Cari about the baby."

Zoe was about to speak, but the living room grew quiet once the guys entered.

"Fuck y'all in here talking about? Why everybody get quiet and looking all silly and shit?" Zoo asked.

"I was complaining about hauling all this stuff back to Rory's," I lied. Zay stopped picking up trash to look at me. Every time he looked at me, I could see his true feelings. He believed everything I said was a lie, which, in this case, it was, but still.

"Dad, can we show Brad our baby shower present now?" Cari asked excitedly.

"Yeah, you can." Zay went back to cleaning up.

"Come on, ladies, follow me," Cari smiled.

"Cari, where are we going?" I asked as he helped me off the couch the best way he could.

"Just follow me." He grabbed my hand, guiding me up the stairs.

I didn't know whose house this was, and I didn't feel comfortable roaming around it. Walking to the top of the stairs, I realized all the doors to the rooms were closed, but one, in particular, caught my attention: the pink door that read, "Princess Carlee Zay".

"Cari, what's this?" I asked, confused.

"Come see!" He pulled me to the closed door.

Turning the doorknob, my eyes watered as I looked around the beautiful nursery. "Surprise!" Cari yelled.

"Oh my goodness, this is so nice," I cried, walking inside and everyone else followed.

"Daddy and I painted and decorated the room, you like it?"

"Yes, I love it." I hugged him.

"Y'all can come do the triplets nursery next, nephew," Zoo said, coming into the room with an arm full of gifts. Boss, Steel, Zay, and Crash were right behind him, carrying my daughter's gifts in the room as well.

"This is nice. I wish I was having a girl," Ramsey smiled, sitting in the rocking chair.

"I was wondering whose house we were in." Rory sat on the footrest.

"Daddy bought this house for us. He said we needed a bigger house; we needed more room for my baby sister," Cari beamed. Still, Zay said nothing. His silence was annoying me.

"Come on, let me show you your room." Cari grabbed my hand.

"Y'all go ahead, I'll stay right here and monitor the guys," Ramsey said, getting comfortable in the rocking chair. Those babies were wearing her out.

"So, let me get this straight. Zay bought you a whole house but hasn't said a word to you," my sister whispered in my ear.

"Listen, at this point, no one is more confused than I am right now," I said, following Cari down the hall.

"This is your room," Cari said, opening the door. My face lit up. The room was so big and beautiful. The king size bed looked comfortable, and I was ready to kick off my shoes and climb right on up in the bed.

Walking around the room, I admired it. Peeking inside the walk-in closet, I was praying I saw Zay's belongings inside. I was hoping we were sharing this room. I tried to hide my excitement when I noticed his clothes hanging on one side of the huge closet.

I was exhausted after walking around this whole house. "I have one more thing to show you, and you're going to love it," Cari said, pulling me to what I guessed was the basement.

"Cari, I'm tired, I can't do any more steps," I whined. Being eight months pregnant was no joke.

"Please, trust me, it will be worth it."

"Okay!" I whined, following his lead.

"Oh my goodness." The waterworks began the moment I stepped off the last step.

"Aw, that's so nice." Rory admired the basement.

"Sister, I've been worried about you, but it's clear you're doing well. This house is beautiful, but I'm talking about the thought that Zay put into it. A man who believes in your dreams and sees your vision is a keeper." My sister hugged me.

"I agree," Summers smiled.

"So, I take it you love your art studio?" Cari cheesed.

"Our art studio." I hugged him. "I see you been down here working." I noticed an unfinished painting.

"Yeah, I'm working on something for my sister. I can't wait to meet her."

"She's going to love you." I pulled him in for a hug.

"Well, way to go, Zay. Way to make everyone else's baby shower gifts look like something from Dollar Tree," Rory joked as we made our way back up to the living room.

"Well, it's getting late, baby sister, I got to get going."

"Okay," I said sadly. "It was nice seeing you."

"Don't sound so sad. I'll be calling you tomorrow so we can make plans to have a sister day."

"Okay." I cheered up.

"It was nice meeting everyone," Shani said after hugging me.

"We're out of here, too. Come on, baby," Steel said, grabbing Summers' hand.

"Thanks again, Summers," Zay called out.

"No problem, bro. Goodnight, everyone."

"Come on, Rah, we're out, too. It's time for you and dem boyz to get some rest."

"Thanks, Zay, I really enjoyed myself. You the best brother a girl could ask for." Ramsey hugged him.

"I got you like you got me," he said, hugging her back.

"Boss, you need to be getting home before your crazy bitch shows up. You know she has a tracking device on your car," Rory said, gathering her things.

"Shut the fuck up, I'm going home with you."

"Come here, Cari. Give me a hug bye, I'm about to go." I stretched my arms out to him to come to me. He looked confused and disappointed.

"Where the fuck do you think you're going?" Zay finally spoke to me. I could tell my sister was taken aback by his aggressive tone.

"Home. My ride's about to leave."

"You are home." His voice dripped with attitude.

"Did you really think I would stay here after the way you've been treating me all day?" It's like everyone stopped there plans to leave to hear his response.

"How have I treated you today? I haven't said shit to you." He raised his voice.

"My point exactly. You haven't said shit to me in weeks, and when you did, it was, 'I want a blood test.'"

"Everyone can go, she's good."

"Ba'Cari, I love you. I'll call you tomorrow," I said, following after Rory.

"Bradleigh, don't make me show my ass in front of my son." His hands rested on my belly because I was now wrapped up in his arms while he whispered in my ear. His touch was gentle, but his words, not so much.

"Girl, call me tomorrow," Rory called out.

"She'll do you one better; you'll see her tomorrow when we come over to get her shit."

"Okay," Rory said.

"All right, everyone, thanks for coming, drive safe." Zay stood at the door, seeing everyone off.

"Cari, go get ready for bed," Zay said, locking the door.

"Okay," he said, running off to his room.

I wanted to curse this disrespectful bastard out. He had turned the light out in the living room as if I wasn't standing there. I was now standing in the middle of a dark room as he made his way upstairs. Taking a deep breath, I made my way upstairs to my new bedroom. I was ready to shower and go to bed.

Walking into the master bedroom, I saw that my night clothes were already laid out on the bed, so I went to draw my bath water, but it was already awaiting me as well. Zay really wanted to be this asshole, but he really didn't have it in him. I soaked in the water, allowing the aches and pains from the day to wash away.

After getting out, drying off and putting on my clothes, I walked into the room, and Zay was lying in bed, watching ESPN. Walking out the room and down the hall to Cari's room, I peeked inside. "Movies until bed?" I questioned. Hopping out of his bed with his sketchbook, he followed me down the hall. Cari hopped on the bed while I walked around to Zay's side of the bed. He watched me while I picked up the remote from his nightstand.

Clicking the OnDemand button, I allowed Cari to pick the movie. "I was watching that," Zay spoke, bothered.

"Don't find your voice now, nigga." I rolled my eyes. I hated to get out of character, but my feelings were hurt.

When Cari suggested I lay in the middle because he wanted to be closer to the lamp, so he could see while drawing, I got annoyed. I didn't want to be next to Zay.

That was short lived because I didn't make the opening credits of the movie before I was knocked out. I woke up from my sleep because the TV sounded like the volume was on a hundred. Feeling around for the remote, I realized Ba'Cari was no longer beside me. Turning the TV off, I went to check on Ba'Cari, and he was sound asleep in his bed. Climbing back into my new bed, it felt like heaven. Rolling over, I stared at my handsome baby daddy as he slept. I'd missed him so much over the last few weeks. Moving as close as my belly would allow, I cuddled under him. Not being able to help myself, I pressed my lips against his several times.

Zay's eyes slowly opened, and I slightly smiled. "I love you," I whispered against his lips. Grabbing my face, he pecked my lips before falling back to sleep. Kissing his lips one last time, I rolled over, and like a magnet, Zay pulled my body to his. It didn't take me long to fall back asleep. I was happy to be back in Zay's arms.

ZOO

After a long day of attending the baby shower, I wanted to come and chill with my babies, but Ramsey wasn't having it. She wanted all the baby shower gifts properly put away.

I was finally able to climb my ass in bed after hours of putting all the shit away. I had just recently bought us a five-bedroom house since we needed more space for the triplets. It didn't take long for me to fall asleep. The shit was short-lived, thanks to Ramsey's constant moving and whining in her sleep. Reaching over, I turned on the lamp that sat on the nightstand. I didn't get how she was still asleep as beads of sweat rested on her forehead.

"Aye, baby, wake up." I wiped her forehead; her whole body was sweating. Placing my hand on her belly, I rubbed it, feeling my boys move like crazy.

"Leave me alone, Zouk, I'm sleepy," she whined, pushing me away.

"Baby, you're moving way too fucking much, you're sweating, and crying in your sleep. Are you in any pain?" I asked, concerned, helping her sit up in bed.

"Of course, I'm in pain, Zouk! I have three tiny humans growing inside me. Come help me up, I need to use the bathroom."

"I knew it was a bad idea letting you go to the baby shower; too much damn excitement. I realized your ankles and feet were swollen." Walking around to her side of the bed, I carefully helped her up. "My big baby!" I smiled, kissing her lips.

"Don't call me big, Zouk!" she whined, pushing me away from her. Walking into the bathroom, she slammed the door. It was crazy how insecure she was about her body. I made it my business to tell her how beautiful she was to me on a daily, but what I said meant nothing; all she saw was all the weight she had picked up carrying my boys.

"Zoo!" Ramsey yelled from the bathroom. I could hear the panic in her voice.

I quickly rushed to the bathroom because the panic in her voice scared me. "What's wrong, baby?"

"I need to go to the hospital, something doesn't feel right." Tears ran down my baby's pretty, fat face.

"Take deep breaths, baby. We knew this day was coming, so don't panic." I tried to remain calm for her sake.

"Zoo, I'm scared."

"Let's just get you to the hospital."

After getting dressed and grabbing the hospital bag, we were on the road.

The whole way to the hospital, I had tunnel vision. If I hadn't been reading up on the delivery birth of triplets, I would have been just as fucked as Ramsey right now. She cried the whole way to the hospital. I was grateful when we got there. Helping Ramsey into the hospital, I got her registered, and Ramsey was quickly roomed.

"Baby, I'm scared. My C-section wasn't scheduled until my thirty-six-week mark; I'm only thirty-four weeks, Zoo, it's too soon."

"Baby, calm down, we talked about this. This is what I tried to prepare you for. We knew our chance of delivering this soon."

"I want my nanna, Zoo. Please get my nanna here." Ramsey cried like a baby.

I hated to call Nanna at one in the morning, but I knew Ramsey wouldn't stop raising hell until I did. I also knew if I called Nanna for

Ramsey, she would come running. Zoe was out hoeing but was willing to cut his time short to pick up Nanna.

Things began to move quickly after Ramsey's water broke and she got her epidural. I wanted to fuck someone up; I hated watching my baby cry out in pain. These contractions were kicking her ass. It seemed like everything that could go wrong with carrying triplets, did.

I wanted to raise hell, but I had to remember I had to stay strong for Ramsey. Seemed like every time I looked up, they were poking or prying at my baby.

That was hours ago. It was now 5:45 a.m., and she had given birth to my baby boys. The whole experience was scary as fuck, seeing that they were born at thirty-four weeks old. Not only was I afraid for the triplets' health, but I also had to worry about Ramsey as well. Her blood pressure was through the roof. The doctor had to perform an emergency C-section because one of the babies were positioned wrong.

Not only were my little niggas barely weighing in, but Zouk Jr. and Zane also had trouble breathing on their own, and Zion was born smaller than his brothers. Zouk and Zane weighed four pounds, and Zion only weighed three. Zouk, Zane, and Zion's organs weren't quite mature, so my mans had to stay in the hospital until they got their weight up. I had faith my boys would come out strong, after all, they were the product of Zouk "Zoo" Taylor, and their mother was a soldier as well.

I didn't think I could love that girl any more than I did, but after tonight, a nigga was wrong. I loved love, don't get me wrong, but I had never loved a girl as much as I loved Ramsey. From the jump, I wanted to do right by her, and I hated myself for sometimes coming up short and hurting her. She and my kids were my world, and I was ready to give them all my last name.

16

ZAY

Things between Bradleigh and I were still the same. Yeah, we were back living under the same roof, but it didn't change the fact that I didn't have shit to say to her. The whole situation was fucked up from start to finish. Everything in me wanted to be a fuck nigga and say fuck Bradleigh and the baby, but I just couldn't do it. Even if I truly believed Bradleigh's baby wasn't mine, I couldn't let the people in my family take care of them because I was the one who had brought them into the fold. No matter how pissed off I was with Bradleigh, I couldn't turn my back on her.

The baby shower was a few weeks ago, and the energy in my house was suffocating, so I decided to get out and meet up with my niggas.

Zoo's triplets were still in NICU so he could use the drink more than me right now. Boss had to deal with Rory on a daily, so he deserved a drink or two as well.

"Are you ready, nigga?" Steel asked, bringing my attention away from all my problems I replayed in my head.

"Ready for what?" I asked.

"Nigga, you're about to be a father soon."

"Am I?" I looked around at Boss, Zoo, Steel, and Crash.

"Nigga, cut the bullshit. You been punishing that girl for weeks for a situation you played a role in as well."

"Zoo, don't start your shit." I shot my brother a look.

"Someone needs to call you on your shit." He shot me the same exact look.

"That person can't be you, my nigga. You're terrible at handling certain situations. If the shoe was on the other foot, your ass would be raising hell."

"Nah, I'm growing, my nigga. Hell yeah, I would be pissed, but with all the shit I've been going through these last few years, I would stop and think: is this shit I'm doing worth losing my girl and kid over? Do you honestly think you didn't play a role in this, and do you really believe the baby isn't really yours?"

"I don't know." I tossed back my shot.

"Nigga, you know, or you wouldn't have told Ba'Cari. Nigga, you bought a five-bedroom house. Not for you and Cari; you bought it as a baby shower gift for Bradleigh to make sure she and the baby are comfortable and happy. Your intentions were good, but that girl hates being there because you go out of your way to make her feel uncomfortable all because you got too fucking loaded. We keep telling you the shit happened, and deep down inside, you know the shit is true as well, or you wouldn't have named Carlee after you. You know you love Bradleigh's young ass, so you better chill before you lose her. Niggas don't be satisfied until their baby mama find a nigga like me and their kids is calling a new nigga daddy. Bradleigh is in her prime. Don't play yourself, Zay; she's a good girl."

My blood was boiling at the thought of Bradleigh entertaining another nigga, yet I knew Zoo had a good point. I was now throwing back my fifth shot.

"See, nigga, that's your problem right there. Don't get mad if shorty sitting down the bar pops up nine months from now carrying your baby. This situation should've taught you to learn your limits." Boss pushed the shot the bartender had placed in front of me away.

"You niggas is real judgmental tonight. Boss, nigga, don't forget your whipped ass is about to have a one-night stand baby as well."

"Nigga, I'll beat your ass if you call my son a one-night stand baby again!" Boss looked like he was ready to fight. "Unlike Rory, Brad didn't purposely trap your ass. Still knowing Rory was on some shady shit, you see where I'm at. I had to realize, although Rory came in knowing she had fucked up intentions, I played a role in how shit went down as well; I never thought once to strap up."

"All right, you niggas can chill with the counseling and shit. I came out to forget about my problems."

"Nigga, being here, downing bottles is the root and the cause," Crash added.

"Brad isn't a fucking victim," I yelled, pissed.

"Neither are you, nigga! Come to terms that y'all both fucked up and move on. I'm tired of seeing you mope around like a lovesick little bitch," Zoo spoke.

"Fuck you, niggas. Bradleigh deserves this treatment."

"Okay, we won't say shit else, nigga. We're going to let your dumb ass do you."

"Thank you. Just focus on your shit, I got mine covered."

After chilling with the boys for a few more hours, I finally made my way home. Yeah, I was giving them shit about giving me advice, but I had heard everything those niggas were saying. Although they all had good points, I was too stubborn to give in. Ego was a motherfucker.

It was going on three in the morning when I came stumbling through my house. Cari wasn't home, so I strolled past his room. Although I couldn't stand Bradleigh right now, I couldn't wait to get in bed and lay up under Brad and Carlee.

Not giving a fuck if Brad was asleep or not, I turned our bedroom light on. I quickly grew pissed off seeing our king size bed was empty, and still made. Backing out the room, I checked the nursery before checking the spare bedrooms. All empty.

"She stays fucking trying me!" I yelled as I made my way down to the basement.

If she wasn't down there working, I was going to murder her ass. Coming up empty again, I pulled out my phone to call her. I didn't understand why her nine-month pregnant ass wasn't home in bed at three in the morning. I called Brad's phone over five times without receiving any answer. I felt like it was déjà vu calling Boss' number again.

"Yo!" Boss answered.

"I need you to find my dumb-ass baby mama. Can you track her shit for me?"

"No need, she's here in our guest room."

"I'm on my way."

"Nigga, we told you so!"

"Fuck off my line!" I said before hanging up.

Grabbing my keys, I made my way back out the door to get Bradleigh's run away ass.

~

"WHY ARE YOU HERE?"

"Why every time you run away, you ask that dumb-ass question? Why do you think I'm here?"

"Listen, Za'Cari, I'm done. You don't believe Braylen is yours, so why do we keep going around in the same circle about it? I'm willing to move on; I refuse to force your hand."

"Who the fuck is Braylen?"

"My daughter. Why would I name her after a man who doesn't believe he's the father? Zay, just go home! Whatever we had is done."

"Brad, stop trying my fucking patience. Get the fuck up and get your shit!" I yelled, pinching the bridge of my nose.

"No! Zay, just leave. I'm done. How long did you think I would sit around and allow you to treat me like shit?" I could tell she was fed up. Shit between us was all fucked up. "I'm staying here. You act like you don't want me there anyway so I won't be. You only want me to communicate with you when the baby is born? One can only hope if I feel up to it. Zay, I don't want or need you, so just go," she yelled, fed up.

Hearing her say she didn't want or need me had me ready to put my hands on her.

"You see the thanks you give me for holding your ass down?" I yelled. "All you do is lie and act so fucking ungrateful. The foundation you're standing on now, I fucking built, but you don't need me? When you had nobody, I was fucking there."

"So, you feel like that gives you the right to treat me like you do? We both played a role in this fucked up situation. I've owned up to that on my end, but it's you that has a problem owning your shit.

"I'm nine months pregnant, I'm beyond stressed and tired, Zay. At this point, I just want peace, and right now, I can't get that being around you. I will be staying here until I find a place for me and the baby. I will contact you after I have the baby so you can get a blood test done. After that, we can determine how we will co-parent. Until then, you're right; we have nothing to talk about. Come on so I can show you out," she said, getting up from the bed. From the look on her face, I could tell I couldn't convince her to come home, and the conversation was over. Nothing else needed to be said or could be said to move us past this point.

Boss didn't try to hide the fact that he was all in our conversation. "Nigga, we told you so!" He shook his head.

"Brad," I tried to speak, but she raised her hand to stop me from speaking.

"I'll call you after I go into labor."

"Call me before."

"I said I'll call you after. No need to see all the extra if you strongly feel she's not yours. Bye, Zay. Boss, can you lock up after him? I'm going back to bed." Brad walked off, leaving me standing there, fuming with anger.

"Shut the fuck up, Boss!" I cut him off before he could start with the I told you so bullshit. I left before he could speak. This whole situation was driving me crazy.

BRADLEIGH

Sadly, with all the shit I had talked, I didn't have any plans on going out to look for a new place for the baby and me. I was squatting out at Rory's until Zay came to his senses. Sadly, it was going on weeks, and he was still on his shit like he didn't care. I wanted so badly not to care, but I just couldn't. I really wanted us to be a family. Call me young and dumb, but I wasn't giving up.

I also wasn't going to let Zay treat me like trash, no matter how much I loved and wanted him. That was why I had made the huge scene a couple weeks ago, and I meant every word. I still had plans to name my daughter Carlee because I knew Zay was her father, and because Ba'Cari had named my baby girl that. I just said I wouldn't name her Carlee to piss Zay off. See, we had been doing a lot of tit for tat lately, trying to one-up each other with hurt.

Christmas, New Year and also my due date had passed, and I was very much still pregnant. My January ninth due date had come and gone. I had lost sight of my feet several months ago, and I was passed over being pregnant after weeks of practically begging my doctor to induce me.

I had no plans of telling Zay I was getting induced. For the last few days, I stressed about being alone while I delivered, but thankfully, I didn't have to worry because my sister Shani and Rory were sitting right by my hospital bedside. I knew how uncomfortable Rory had to be, considering we had already been waiting for hours, so that was why I told her she didn't have to be here by my side, but she insisted. Our bond was just like that. Rory was my big sister, always looking out for my best interest.

When I first arrived at the hospital, I was admitted and placed in my room, and the nurse wasted no time hooking me up to a bag of fluid and a fetal monitor. My nerves started to kick in when the nurse gave me my first dose of medication to begin the induction.

The beginning of my induction started at five p.m., and I was tired of staring at four walls, waiting for something to happen, so I fell asleep.

I was in and out, thanks to the nurses being in and out my room, checking on my progress. I was thankful I was able to get a few hours of uninterrupted sleep, and by the time I woke up, it was six a.m. My sister slept on the couch in the corner of my room, Rory was gone, and Zay was now sitting by my side.

"Hey, Mommy, how are you feeling?" my nurse asked, pulling my attention away from Zay. He still looked as if he didn't believe my daughter was his and someone had forced him to be here.

"Good, ready to get this little lady out of there." I smiled down at my stomach excitedly at the thought of holding my baby girl in my arms.

"How's your pain level on a scale of one to ten?" she asked, looking at the fetal monitor before making eye contact with me.

"No labor pains, just the normal I-have-a-tiny-human-growing-inside-of-me pains," I giggled.

"Really?" she asked, shocked.

"Yes, why, is something wrong?" I asked in a panic.

"No, not necessarily, it's just your contractions are hitting four or five minutes apart. You sure you don't feel any pain?"

"No, I don't feel a thing."

"I would like to check to see how much you've dilated." I laid uncomfortably as the nurse checked my cervix. I was starting to overthink. I had only had sex a few times, and now I was about to push a baby out when it came time.

"Okay, Doctor Greggs will be in to break your water to see if that will move things along." She smiled before exiting my room.

After thirty minutes of awkward silence filling my hospital room, Doctor Greggs came in to break my water.

After Doctor Greggs left, my sister Shani tried to lighten the mood in the room by telling me how Crash wouldn't let up on trying to get with her. I was laughing at the demands she was hitting him with to be with her.

The mood in my room took another turn when the contractions hit. Ten minutes after my water was broke, my contractions moved right into my lower back. Ramsey had warned me about how intense lower back contractions were, and boy were these motherfuckers intense.

"Get this little girl out of me!" I cried, grabbing onto the bed rail as another contraction hit.

Zay no longer wore a pissed off look on his face; he now sported a concerned look.

Walking over to me, Zay rubbed my back. "Move over." Sliding over, I gave him enough room to sit on my bed. Zay rubbed my back as another contraction hit a couple minutes later.

"Zay, I'm so glad you're here. I didn't want to do this by myself," I cried, wrapping my arms around his waist, hugging him tightly. "She's yours, I swear to you! I love you too much to play with you like that. I just want us to be a family. Cari and Carlee deserve it, and so do we.

"You and the kids are all I have! When I first saw you again after that night we spent together, I was afraid to reveal the truth because I didn't understand how to explain. As time passed, I still didn't know how to tell you because I was afraid of this very reaction. I fell in love with the man you are, the father you are. The bond you have with Cari, I want for our daughter. Can we agree that we both fucked up and move on, please?" I cried out as another contraction hit harder. I was practically begging Zay to move on from this fucked up situation.

I needed to feel his love and support. I couldn't read his facial expression, and I was afraid he would turn me down again.

Leaning forward, Zay passionately kissed my lips. I guess he had missed me as much as I had missed him.

"What the fuck, Brad?" Zay whined as I bit down roughly on his bottom lip. These contractions were a killer.

"I'm sorry!" I cried as I tried a few breathing exercises, hoping that would take some of the pain away. "I'm hungry. I've been here for hours, I want food."

"Brad, you know you can't have any food until after you have the baby."

I was praying my body quickly got with the program. The last time the nurse checked, I was dilating slowly. I had been in labor for hours, about fourteen, to be exact. The pain was getting worse by the minute, and I wanted this to be over. It felt like I had been having contractions for hours before my nurse entered my room.

"Hey, Mommy, I'm going to check you again." I didn't want to be touched, but I allowed her to do her job. "Well, Mom, it looks like you're about seven centimeters. You're far enough along to get an epidural."

"Yes, please, hurry! I can't take the pain, and I'm hungry."

"Okay, I'll get Doctor Greggs up here." She smiled at me before leaving the room.

For forty-five minutes, I cried out in pain, waiting for the doctor to come give me an epidural.

"Hello, Ms. Lambert, sorry for the delay. Doctor Greggs was rushed into an emergency surgery. I'm Doctor Kass, I will be administering your epidural. Ms. Lambert, do you mind sitting up straight for me," Doctor Kass spoke while the nurse set up what was needed for the epidural. With the help of Zay, I sat up straight in my hospital bed.

"Okay, Ms. Lambert, lean all the way forward for me and be perfectly still," Doctor Kass instructed.

"What are you about to do with that big-ass needle?" Zay asked defensively, causing me to quickly turn around.

"Ms. Lambert, I need you to lean forward and be very still." Nervously, I did what I was told.

"I see that you're nervous, so I'll walk you through this. First, I'm going to feel down your spine to select a point," he said, touching my lower back.

"Now that I've found the spot, I'm going to mark—" Cutting him off, I screamed.

"Relax, Ms. Lambert, it's just a pen," he chuckled, and Shani did the same. Zay's face never changed; he was just as concerned about the needle as I was. "I'm marking the spot," he said, trying to mark the spot again. "Now I'm going to numb the area," he said, and I felt the pinch of the needle going into my back and the stinging of the medication. The pinch and the stinging were light work compared to my contractions.

"Now I'm going to insert the epidural needle."

"Something doesn't feel right, I need to push," I cried.

"No pushing yet, Ms. Lambert. I need you to stay completely still as I insert the epidural needle."

"You're okay, baby, I'm here." Zay held my hand. The epidural kicked in fast, and I felt great.

After being checked, sure enough, I was ten centimeters dilated. My baby girl was ready to meet us.

Doctor Kass couldn't position himself in between my legs good before Carlee's head came sliding out.

Shani cheered in excitement, happy to witness the birth of her niece. Zay watched in amazement as they cleaned her off and suctioned her nose and mouth. I was anxious to hold my baby, but something wasn't right. Carlee wasn't crying, and I quickly started to panic.

"Is she okay?" I nervously asked.

"She's fine!" Doctor Kass smiled, and seconds later, Carlee Zay took her first breath. Hearing the sounds of her cries had my heart filled with love.

Wrapping her up, the nurse laid her on my chest. I kissed all over her tiny face.

"Hey, mommy's baby!" I cried tears of joy.

"She's so beautiful!" Zay said before kissing her forehead.

"She is. I love her so much already." I wiped my tears, overwhelmed with emotions. Carlee looked exactly like the beautiful little girl in my dreams. The greatest blend of Zay and me.

Opening her eyes, she looked at me, and in that moment, I realized everything I had gone through with Zay was well worth it, and to have this perfect little girl who laid in my arms, I would do it all over again.

17

RORY

I guess since I had stayed in everyone's business, they called me in to bring this home. I guess I'll start with what's going on between Boss and me since we keep shit popping.

I gave birth to my handsome baby boy, Brody Braxton Bells, on March tenth. I loved him with everything in me. The feeling I longed for when I first got home, I found in him like I knew I would, and surprisingly, I found the feeling I longed for in Boss as well. We fought like crazy, but we loved even harder. What I thought would be a one-night stand was something I wanted for a lifetime. As crazy as it sounds, Boss and I just clicked.

Kiana was still running around, pressed, and I understood why. How Boss had played her was wrong, and I guess I played a huge part as well, so I could sympathize with her just a little. I could admit I was selfish, and Boss and Brody were who I wanted. Boss and I had decided to make our relationship really official, and before y'all ask, no, I wasn't afraid of him doing me like he had done Kiana because Boss knows I'm with the shit. He knows if he even thought about playing me, my gun would do the talking.

RAMSEY AND ZOO were living happily ever after with their five kids. The triplets were home, healthy, and the growing boys were doing well. My sister looked tired as hell, raising five kids, but I could tell she was happy. Her kids and Zoo are her world, and she deserved the life she was now living after all the hell Lance had put her through. Zoo worshipped the ground my sister walked on, even more so now that she had given him something he longed for as well. The way he loved my sister, my niece, and nephews, I often forgot he could be the world's biggest asshole.

Zay and Brad still had their fair share of ups and downs, thanks to Zay not being able to let go of the past when he got pissed off. That nigga had real deal trust issues. Although Zay couldn't deny Carlee if he wanted to, Brad still made sure to get a paternity test done. That was why she allowed Zay to talk his shit. Brad was crazy in love, not just with Zay, but with her kids as well. After her parents found out her sister Shani was back in contact with her, they made good on their promise and cut her off. It was crazy what her parents were willing to go through to hide her pregnancy and even sadder that the members of their church had no clue who they were following. Shani seemed unbothered by her parents' decision, living her life with Lil' C and Crash. After giving him the runaround, she finally gave him a chance.

WHEN MY SISTER first told me about Summers approaching her at the hospital, I wasn't quite sure what her motives were. In the past, a lot of bitches had come crazy to Ramsey behind Lance's sorry, no-good ass, our own damn sister included, so I didn't know how I felt about her coming around. I was glad she wasn't a bitter baby mama because I now looked at Summers as my sister. She had this positive spirit about her that my crazy ass needed. Steel knew what he had in Summers, and that was why it didn't come as a surprise when he dropped down to one knee and proposed. He'd been asking her to have his baby, and sadly, like Ramsey, Summers was damaged from all the bullshit Lance had put her through.

When Steel changed her last name, Summers changed her mind, birthing a beautiful baby girl. Their little family is family goals.

AFTER JEN WAS SENTENCED, it was fuck her life and anyone else who ever crossed us. Blood or not, her ass meant nothing to me, and I think I could speak for everyone when I said that. Sadly, that didn't stop her delusional ass from reaching out. Convicted and all, Jen was still holding on to her innocence, still blaming Zoo for her problems. In court, Jen's new story was Zoo had paid Nicki off to testify against her and Lance. By her words, he also coached Luna's testimony. Nobody was fucking with Jen's ass, not even my nanna. Jen would do those fourteen years alone.

Lance had to be losing his shit in jail because he had mother-fuckers reaching out to Summers and Ramsey to see "his" kids. We all knew he was doing this to get under Summers and Ramsey's skin. Zoo and Steel weren't feeling how Lance was still trying to bully them from jail and let's just say Lance won't be seeing the kids at all, or anyone else, out of his left eye ever again after the damage a few of Zoo's niggas behind bars handed to him.

Minus the minor bullshit, I guess you could say life was good for us all, but don't close the book just yet, there's more...

THE NEXT GENERATION
LUCHI

Lil' C, Journee and I were speeding through the streets of Downtown Louisville, and the welling sound of sirens and the red, white and blue flashing lights had my adrenaline pumping. We'd been doing this shit for a while, and today, our luck had finally run its course.

"Nigga, move this motherfucker!" Journee yelled in a panic. Hearing my brother lose his shit did something to my mental. I was the reason we were in this stolen car on a high-speed chase with the police.

It was my idea to join this car theft ring. I had a name on the streets because of who my father was, and now I wanted to build a name for myself. My parents had a vision for my life, but a nigga had other plans. I wasn't interested in going to college, but I had graduated high school to satisfy my parents. My goal was to be the man on these streets, and my boys shared the same vision. Stealing cars was just the start, and the way these cops were on our ass, it would be our quick end.

"We need a fucking plan," Lil' C yelled, looking out the back window of the BMW truck we had stolen.

"The best chance we have is to lose these motherfuckers and

run!" I looked in the rearview mirror to see how I could shake their ass.

"Cut through here!" Journee yelled. I quickly made a sharp right, shooting through a narrow alley. The police didn't make the turn in time, causing me to breathe a little easier. Making a left, I shot back in the same direction we had stolen the car from. We were about to ditch this bitch and hideout.

"I'm going to drive a few blocks. One of y'all hop out, and we'll meet back at my spot."

"Naw, nigga, we're sticking together." Journee looked at me crazy from the passenger seat.

"Banks, we don't have time for that; we need to split the fuck up. There will be a better chance of us getting away. Come on, one of you niggas hop out!" I yelled in a panic.

"Lil' C, hop out, bro because I'm not leaving my brother. If he getting caught up, we're going down in this bitch together."

"I feel the same way, nigga, so if we're hopping out this bitch, we're doing it together."

"Well, let's shake this motherfucker, but we need to make a split once we hop out," I yelled, looking around before putting the car in park.

Hopping out, we all made a run for it in separate ways. I could hear the sirens get louder, and I prayed we all got away. Cutting through a few houses, I decided to hide under a porch until I heard the sirens pass.

"Fuck, fuck, fuck!" I yelled, frustrated. Looking around, I emerged from underneath the porch. Looking around, I realized I wasn't too far from my house.

Wanting to make it home safe, I decided to run between houses to get home. I refused to let them catch me because I decided to run out in the open on the main streets.

I was blocks away from my house when a car pulled up beside me in the alley. I was praying it wasn't an unmarked police car.

"Come on, bro, hop in!" Journee yelled from the passenger side window of another nice car. Confused, I quickly hopped in the back seat.

"Shorty, make a right!" Journee focused on the street, and I had a feeling he was looking for Lil' C.

Riding up several blocks, shorty drove slowly, creeping up the block pass all the flashing lights. I didn't understand why Lil' C was caught by the stolen truck.

Thank God shorty had an amazing tint job. It was like Lil' C could feel our presence as he made eye contact with the car. The cops had him pinned against the cop car in handcuffs.

"Fuck!" Journee screamed in frustration. We were both feeling the same way. Shit was going all bad. "Shorty, get us away from here."

"Shit, man!" I felt like tearing shit up.

"Where am I taking you?" Shorty briefly looked over at Journee.

My brother gave her directions while I sat in the back seat, stuck. Shit wasn't supposed to be like this, yet I understood this was a part of the game. I didn't know how we would explain this shit to our parents.

"Come on, Luchi. Come on, nigga, let's go!" Journee yelled, grabbing my attention. We were parked in front of my family's home.

Looking around to make sure the coast was clear, I hopped out. Going through my pocket, I searched for my door keys.

"No need, nigga, come on in!" My Aunt Rory opened the door with the craziest look on her face before I could locate my keys.

"Dude, where the fuck y'all been?" my dad asked. I didn't like how damn near every member of my family was lined up at the front door, looking like they were ready to attack.

"Out playing ball," I lied.

"Where is Cordae?" my dad asked, walking up on me.

"He met some girl at the park," I lied, trying to avoid eye contact with my twin. I knew hearing that would hurt my sister, but for the moment, I needed to cover our ass.

I didn't see my daddy's punch coming until it was too late. "Nigga, you're just going to lie to my motherfucking face? Nigga, who the fuck you take me as? Don't shit pop with mine without me knowing. You should know I got eyes and ears every motherfucking where!" he yelled, raining blow after blow. I wanted to fight back, but I didn't want those types of problems with Zouk Taylor. "Bitch, you out here stealing like I don't bust my ass for mine."

Hearing my brother crying out in pain, I knew he was receiving the same treatment from Steel that I was getting from my dad.

"Do you not understand I got eyes and ears every-fucking-where?" my dad repeated while he beat my ass.

"Tag me in, Zoo!" My Aunt Ro jumped around. "Luchi, I'll beat your ass before I allow you to stress my sister out!" she yelled, helping my father beat my ass.

So much was going on all at once. I could hear my mama cursing me out, Luna sat on the couch, crying, probably because she knew Lil' C had gotten knocked, and Crash looked like he was ready to snap as he paced back and forth. Summers was raising the same amount of hell as my mom, and Ba'Cari looked disappointed. On many occasions, he tried to talk us out of stealing cars. The money was good, and I enjoyed the rush. My brothers, sisters and little cousins stood around, crying because of all the chaos. Shit only got worse.

"Freeze!" the police yelled with guns drawn on my family.

SHAWTY CRAVING HIS LOVE
SHE'S HIS RIDER

Coming Soon 2018...

CPSIA information can be obtained
at www.ICGtesting.com
Printed in the USA
LVOW10s2341190118
563260LV00021B/889/P

9 781981 852550